Mike,
I'm giving this disk to you because I promised. But I'd forget about trying the game. It's addictive. This is a bootleg copy, and there's something weird about it. I couldn't get past level three (Mountain Quest) without scaling the roof of my house. The game will suck you in and it won't let go until something awful happens to you. I got it from Eric Gottlieb, and you know <u>his</u> story. And now, look at me. Eric says there's a virus in the program. I think it's cursed. I mean it, Mike. It's no game. It's a nightmare!

Hacker

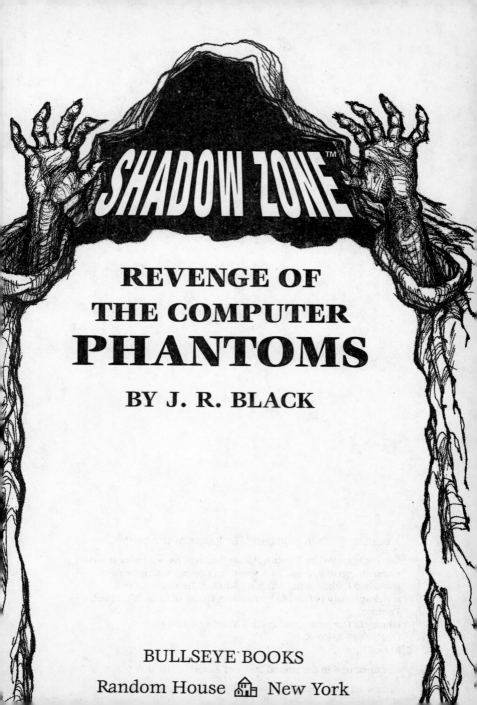

SHADOW ZONE™

REVENGE OF THE COMPUTER PHANTOMS

BY J. R. BLACK

BULLSEYE BOOKS

Random House 🏠 New York

A BULLSEYE BOOK PUBLISHED BY RANDOM HOUSE, INC.

Copyright © 1993 by Twelfth House Productions. All rights reserved
under International and Pan-American Copyright Conventions.
Published in the United States by Random House, Inc., and
simultaneously in Canada by Random House of Canada Limited,
Toronto.
Library of Congress Catalog Card Number: 93-84906
ISBN: 0-679-85407-X
RL: 4.8

Manufactured in the United States of America   10 9 8 7 6 5 4 3 2 1

SHADOW ZONE is a trademark of Twelfth House Productions.

1

Attack of the Pods

Time was running out.

I was surrounded by alien pods that had landed from the sky. The pods opened as they hit the ground, spilling out purple aliens who waddled around like penguins. But unlike penguins, these birds were armed and dangerous. They had wings that could fire off death rays in the time it takes you to sneeze.

And I was their target.

I spun around and zapped the aliens creeping up behind me.

One pod down, five more to go.

I blew up another pod, but now I was running out of ammo. And the crater I'd been hiding in was being eaten away by death rays. Things were not looking good.

It was time to use my last missile, which I'd been saving for an emergency. Use it or lose it! I thought as my palms began to sweat.

I was just about to fire when a hand closed over the small screen of my portable computer, bringing me back to reality...and math class.

"Hey!" I tried to tug the Game Boy away, but it was too late. The aliens had already struck. I was obliterated. Space dust. Game over.

"You messed up my game," I said, looking up. Round glasses and a grim frown stared back at me. Yikes. I tried to bail myself out. "I mean, uh, you shouldn't, uh, creep up on people like that, Mrs. Fernandez."

I couldn't see her eyes behind the glare of her glasses. "*You* should be doing the math exercise, Mr. Willis," she said.

The room was silent. Faces loomed behind Mrs. Fernandez as the other sixth-graders turned around to watch. Kids can smell it when the teacher is moving in for a kill.

"But I did the assignment, ma'am," I said, pointing to the notebook. I'd aced the stupid exercise with time to spare.

"Then you should be working on tomorrow's exercise." Mrs. Fernandez put her hand out. "Give me the game."

I held tight to the Game Boy and started talking a mile a minute. "Please don't take it, Mrs. F. I *did* finish the assignment. And computers *are* educational. But if you have problems with that,

I won't use it in this class again. I promise you—"

"This is the third time this week," she snapped. "Hand it over immediately!"

Defeat. She took the computer and walked back to her desk. I stared at the back of her head, wishing I could land a spitball in her hair. Or better yet, I wished I could zap her into space dust. That would get her off my case.

"Teachers are so unfair," I muttered, waiting for the kids who sat nearby to agree. But they just chewed their pencils and buried their noses deeper in their books.

Devon O'Dell, the suck-up who sits in front of me, turned around and smirked. "I *knew* you'd get caught," he whispered.

Three aisles away, my friend Ben Huxley rolled his eyes and ran a hand over the top of his head. Ben is African-American, and he's got this cool haircut that's totally flat on top. He wants to shave his initials into the hair above his collar, but his mom won't let him.

Ben is my best friend, but Mrs. Fernandez always makes us sit apart. Ben says she's afraid that our combined brain power would blow her out of the classroom. I think it's because we talk.

Finally the tone sounded and school was out. I went to the front of the room to get my Game Boy back, but Mrs. Fernandez had already packed it in her briefcase. "Don't even *think* about it for at least another week," she said.

"Please, Mrs. F," I begged as she marched out the door. "A whole *week*? Seven days of—"

"Give me a hard time and I'll make it two weeks," she said.

That stopped me. It was a losing battle. I turned back to the classroom for my stuff.

"T.B.," Ben said, handing me my notebook.

Translation? Tough break. Ben had a habit of speaking in shorthand.

"Told you not to mess with Mrs. Ferment-head," Ben added. "She's S.T.—psycho teacher."

"That's P.T.," I said. "*Psycho* starts with a p."

"Whatever." He grinned. "Chill, Mikey."

He was the only person who could call me that and get away with it.

"Pull yourself together and forget about the computer," Ben added. "All you ever do these days is hook into a new game. It's like you live on the other side of that screen."

What could I say? It was true. Computer games were way more exciting than the stuff that went on at Woodmont Middle School. "I can't help it if this place is boring," I said.

"Quit complaining and let's go," he said, slinging his knapsack over his shoulder. "We're supposed to be at Vickie's house by three-thirty."

Vickie Goldberg was the third person in our science group. I had forgotten that we'd agreed to work on our project that afternoon.

"What about the Micro-Chip Club?" I asked.

Ben shrugged. "Blow it off. We have to get this earth science project going. Vickie's mom is letting us build the volcano in their basement."

"Tell Vickie we'll do it some other day," I said. "Hacker promised to give me a copy of *Phantom Quest* today."

"Get it tomorrow," Ben said, nudging my shoulder. "Besides, all you do in that club is sit around and play computer games."

The last thing I needed was a put-down from Ben. "Give me a break. First Mrs. Fernandez, now you." I raised my arms as if asking the ceiling, "Doesn't anyone care about what *I* want to do?"

Silence. "Fine," Ben said, heading toward the door. "But don't blame me when you flunk out of science."

I felt bad. Maybe I shouldn't have stuck Ben alone with Vickie Goldberg. But he could have come with me if he wanted. Besides, we had two whole weeks before our project was due. They were probably just going to sit around and talk about who got detention and who liked who.

The bad feeling didn't go away when I turned

into the computer lab. Hacker was a no-show. In fact, only a few members had turned up, probably because it was pouring rain outside.

"Too bad about Hacker, isn't it?" said the kid beside me. It was John Miluski. John was a computer hound who reminded me of a big poodle. Maybe it was his curly hair and long, pointed nose.

"What do you mean?" I asked, shoving my books onto a desk.

"Didn't you hear?" he asked. I shook my head, and he went on, "He fell off the roof of his house this morning. Landed smack on the back patio. He's in the hospital with a broken leg."

My heart sank. It was awful news. "What was Hacker doing on the roof?"

"Beats me." John shrugged. "Who can figure that kid out? He's been even weirder than usual recently."

Thunder rumbled as John turned back to his terminal. I opened my disk carrier and pulled out a floppy. It looked like I was going to be stuck playing *Pack-Rat* for a few more weeks. I booted up and started the old game.

My man was bouncing through the tunnels, setting rat traps, when someone called my name.

"Sorry to disturb you." It was Mr. Norman,

the club adviser. He was pale and pudgy, kind of like a marshmallow man. His thinning blond hair was combed over a bald spot on top. I tried not to stare at it since Mr. Norman was the best teacher I'd ever had.

"What's up?" I asked.

He handed me a manila envelope. "Hacker's mom dropped this off in the office. It's for you."

I pushed my glasses up on my nose to read my name on the envelope: *Mike Willis*. Underneath it was marked PERSONAL and underlined twice. It was strange to get a package through the school office, but I was pretty sure I knew what was inside.

"Thanks," I told Mr. Norman. As soon as he started back to his desk, I ripped open the flap and looked inside. There was a disk and a note.

I pulled out the disk. *Phantom Quest!* Hacker had come through—broken leg and all! I unfolded Hacker's note, which was written in a rushed scrawl.

> Mike,
> I'm giving this disk to you because I promised. But I'd forget about trying the game. It's addictive. This is a bootleg copy, and there's something weird about it. I couldn't get past

level three (Mountain Quest) without scaling the roof of my house. The game will suck you in and it won't let go until something awful happens to you. I got it from Eric Gottlieb, and you know <u>his</u> story. And now, look at me. Eric says there's a virus in the program. I think it's cursed. I mean it, Mike. It's no game. It's a nightmare!

Hacker

2

The Phantom Curse

My throat felt tight. Why was Hacker trying to scare me?

I read the note again. Was it a joke? If so, it wasn't a very funny one, since the guy was laid up in the hospital. And Hacker wasn't one to clown around. I'd known him since the beginning of the school year, and he had yet to crack a smile.

I also knew all about Eric Gottlieb. Everyone did. The story of how he'd almost died during a swim meet had even hit the local paper.

It was during a race at the indoor sports center that someone noticed Eric's body at the bottom of the pool. Eric was legally dead when the lifeguard got him out of the water. Luckily, the paramedics were able to get him breathing.

No one knew how Eric's body got sucked down to the bottom of the pool that way. Ben and I had been really creeped out. But I hadn't heard anything about it being caused by a cursed computer game.

In fact, it was probably just a fluke. I mean, Eric wasn't playing *Phantom Quest* in the pool.

I picked up the game disk. It looked just like every other 3½-inch plastic diskette I'd ever seen. There was no way a program could be cursed. I'd given up on that kind of stuff last summer when I'd caught Ben pushing the pointer across the Ouija board.

I looked back at the screen. The Pack-Rats had squeezed past my traps and were nibbling on my guy's feet. I exited the program and popped out the disk.

I studied the *Phantom Quest* disk. Aw...what the heck!

I pushed in the game disk and booted up. *Are you ready to begin the quest?* The words zipped across the screen. I typed in Y for yes.

A yellow and blue lightning bolt formed the words *Phantom Quest*. Then I was into level one—Ocean Quest. I had to reach a treasure on the ocean floor before the phantom divers caught me.

"What's that?" John asked over my shoulder.

"A new game I'm trying out."

"My cousin had that game," John said, peering at the monitor. "*Phantom Quest,* right?"

I nodded, not taking my eyes off the screen.

"Bootleg or original?" he asked.

"What do *you* think?" I said sarcastically.

There was no way I could save enough money to buy *Phantom Quest*. And my parents were no help. Computers made my mom nervous, and Dad thought I spent too much time indoors.

"Well," John said, "you'd better watch out. The disk could have a glitch in it."

"I know." I'd heard the warnings before. A few clever hackers had created viruses that could sneak in and crash a program. There's always the possibility that a bootleg disk is infected. But no one *I* knew had ever gotten a sick disk.

Meanwhile, level one—Ocean Quest—was going well. I made my diver pick up a giant shell and use it as a shield to fend off a torpedo. Then the coast was clear. I swam to the treasure chest and touched the key to the lock. The chest sprang open and treasure spilled out.

You won quest 1!

"Yes!" I said, as jewels and gold coins floated across the screen.

"Good luck," John said. "My cousin never got past level two."

"Maybe he didn't keep at it long enough."

"No." John was quiet for a second. Then he

added, "He played that game all the time. Non-stop. Until he was buried alive."

"What?" My concentration had been broken. I turned to stare at John. "Are you kidding?"

"I wish I was." John's poodle eyes looked sad. "It happened at a construction site. He fell in a hole, and a bulldozer covered him with dirt. He remembers something pulling him under, like the phantoms in level two of that game."

"Gruesome," I said. "How'd he get out?"

"Someone walking by saw it happen. After that, he gave the game away. Said he'd never use a bootleg disk again. Weird, huh?"

I shivered. That was the third bad-luck story I'd heard today. But how could all these accidents be connected to a computer game?

I wanted to ask John, but he'd already wandered down the aisle to another terminal.

I looked back at the screen just in time to see level two—Earth Quest. Before I could touch the keyboard, a phantom hand snaked through the dirt and tugged my guy down. Everything caved in, crushing my man.

You're dead! the screen told me.

Trying to ignore the queasy feeling in my stomach, I started level two again.

My man was a miner who had to carve his way out of the center of the earth before phantoms pulled him under. As I played, I barely noticed the other kids talking and laughing. Then halfway through the level, the screen went blank.

"Come back!" I groaned. Was this the bug Hacker had mentioned? I ran a check on the diskette and found that two sectors were bad.

"Well, no wonder..." I muttered. Hacker was slipping. I'd have to copy the game onto a good disk. I input the command to copy the program onto the computer's hard drive.

As the program was copying, I looked around the lab. Mr. Norman was grading papers at his desk. The other kids were leaving. No one was paying any attention to me.

The rain still hadn't let up as I started to play the game again. It was time to head home, but I was getting psyched. I'd be the first one in Woodmont, Illinois, to master this game. I wouldn't need to make up a gruesome story as an excuse for defeat!

This time I reached level three—Mountain Quest. My guy had just kicked a phantom over a cliff when I heard Mr. Norman shuffling by. "I'll be back in a minute," he said. "I'm getting some forms from the office."

I nodded, never taking my eyes off the screen. I needed every ounce of concentration just to find footholds in the rock face of the cliff my guy was scaling. And the whole time the phantoms were chasing me, trying to yank me off the mountain.

At last, I reached the peak! When I buried the flag in the snow, the screen flashed me a message. *Nice climbing, Mikey!*

"What?" I thought I saw my name, but it flashed on the screen so fast I couldn't be sure. Maybe I was just delirious that I'd made it to level four—Phantom Quest.

Lightning lit the room as four figures hooded in black appeared on the screen.

Creep city!

They were the phantoms I'd been trying to escape in the first three levels, and they looked like grim reapers...until they ripped off the black hoods to reveal their faces.

Choose your gladiator for the first match.

"None of the choices look too good," I said, and was answered by a rumble of thunder outside. These were not people you'd bring home for dinner. There was a beefy blond guy. There was a rubbery-looking bald man and a squarish man of steel. And the fourth face was a woman with a cruel smile.

I chose the blond guy, whose name was Thor.

Raindrops splattered against the windows,

but I tuned the world out as I tried to figure out level four. It was a gladiator tournament with matches that tested the gladiators' physical strength. You had to choose a gladiator to be your man for each match. Thor seemed pretty good, so I choose him every time. Each match pitted him against the other gladiators, the rejects, who put the black hoods back on when they weren't chosen.

The first match was called the Spider's Web, where the hooded phantoms tried to pull Thor off a web before he reached the top.

Next was a bowling event. The phantoms rolled these giant black balls down a lane, and Thor had to jump and dodge them to avoid getting flattened. He had to stay up for thirty seconds...and the clock was ticking away.

I was stabbing a key, making Thor jump, when lightning struck outside. There was a flash of white, then everything went black...pitch black.

"Not now!" Why did the power always go out at the worst possible times?

I pushed away from the terminal, waiting for my eyes to adjust. If the power was going to be out for a while, I might as well head home. As I stood up, the overhead light blinked on. Then the monitor began to glow red, which was weird because it should have gone back to the black screen.

I dropped into my chair and scooted up to the terminal. If level four was going to continue, I wanted to be ready to play. I was hooked on the game. I could smell victory.

But as I watched, smoke rose from the computer. It was glowing green. My heart began to pound. Was there a fire? Had the *Phantom Quest* program blown the whole system?

A shimmering cloud shot out of the screen. The faces of the gladiators rose from the smoke. Then they faded and lost shape.

"*Very* weird."

The smoke swirled and formed the face of the gladiator I'd chosen—Thor. From the cloud came curly blond hair, icy blue eyes, and a square jaw that was fixed in a permanent sneer. The image was bold and colorful—like a comic book character—but three-dimensional.

I was hallucinating. That was the only explanation.

Unfortunately, Thor was looking more and more solid. His muscular arms formed from the mist. With a grunt, he pulled himself out of the monitor.

He was real...and he was coming after me!

3

Zapped!

The curse was coming true...

My mouth opened, but not even a squeak came out. No one had explained that a phantom would actually come out of the computer to carry out its evil!

Was he going to bury me alive or throw me off a rooftop?

I had to stop him. But what could I do?

An idea hit me while Thor was pulling his huge legs out of the mist. Cut the power and you kill the phantom.

Shaking, I slid my chair closer to the terminal. Heat radiated from Thor's shiny belt buckle as I reached forward and hit the switch. The monitor blinked off, but the phantom gladiator kept growing.

Apparently, he had his own power supply. Was he energized like that annoying battery-powered rabbit on TV? Or did his power come from the lightning outside? I was scratching my head, wondering, when...

Zammmm!

Thor pointed two beefy fingers at me and fired sparks into my chest.

"Ahhh!" The shock sent me reeling backward. My chair wheeled down the aisle as I recoiled in pain. I had a gutful of electricity!

I yanked off my glasses to swipe at the tears that blurred my vision. When I looked up again, Thor was hoisting his feet out of the monitor and springing through the air like a gymnast. The room seemed to rock as he landed squarely on the floor in front of me.

He wore bicycle shorts and a tight neon tank shirt that had to stretch over every muscle. On his head was a set of horns that made him look like a Viking warrior. The guy had a massive head that reminded me of a pit bull.

"Reality," he said, looking around suspiciously, then grinning. "Not bad."

"What are you doing here?" My voice was a nervous squeak. I couldn't believe a character from a computer game was standing before me.

"I've come for you!" he growled. He looked me up and down. "A puny boy. But I know you like games. It's time to play...from now till eternity."

"What do you mean?" I asked, backing away. "Are you going to kill me?" I could just see the headlines now: BOY ELECTROCUTED IN COMPUTER LAB!

"That would be too easy," he said with an evil smile. "I've got something much better in store for you. You're going to play the game, kid. Play it over and over again until..."

"Until what?" Adrenaline shot through my body as I looked from Thor to the computer. Common sense told me to run. Split! But I was frozen, afraid that he'd attack me again. My body still hurt from the first zap.

Thor jumped onto a desk, knocking a keyboard onto the floor. "Where are the others?" he demanded, scoping out the room.

"Others?" I was afraid to tell him that there were probably no other people within shouting distance. I mean, when you're home alone, you're not supposed to admit that to a stranger.

"The Exterminator," he barked out. "Siren. Mongo." When I didn't answer, he leaped off the table and lunged at me. "The other gladiators, boy. Don't tell me you don't even know the game!"

"I just got it today," I choked out as Thor grabbed me by the collar of my shirt. If I answered wrong, he'd probably whip me through

19

the air and toss me around like a wet rag. "But I learn fast."

"Not fast enough. You haven't learned yet that it's not wise to play with a bootleg disk. Now you'll find out about the curse firsthand." He chuckled grimly as he lifted me out of the chair. Then I was staring at the lightning bolt emblazoned on his shirt. It was a good thing he was holding me up, because my knees were shaking.

"You're a shrimp. A weakling," he growled.

So I don't spring out of bed every morning and drop to the floor for twenty push-ups. Nobody's perfect.

"You're right," I admitted, seeing a way out of this monster-man's grip. "I'm just a scrawny kid. You need someone bigger and stronger. So if you want to go back into the computer until a better specimen comes along, that's okay with me."

"You can't weasel out!" he thundered, dropping me down into a chair and pushing me over to the computer. He switched on the terminal and the *Phantom Quest* logo glowed on the screen, casting a maniacal light on Thor's face.

"Play the game!" he barked.

"Now?" I asked in disbelief. Believe me, the last thing I wanted to do was to play that computer game. I wanted to curl into a ball and close my eyes and hope that when I opened them Thor would be gone.

"Play the game," he repeated.

As I sat there trying to keep my lunch down, something weird happened. My fingers began to itch inside. Suddenly, they were tapping keys like crazy.

It was like my hands were controlled by someone else. I was playing the game—whether I liked it or not.

"That's better," Thor said over my shoulder.

I gritted my teeth, trying to stop my fingers, but they just kept flying over the keys. "What are you doing to me?"

"Just play the game," he grumbled.

When we got to level four, Thor leaned closer to the screen. "Hold on a minute," he said. "Let's make sure the others are still there."

Three hooded heads appeared on the screen. When they ripped off their hoods, Thor chortled at the sight of the three gladiators.

"Yes! They're in! I'm out! It's perfect." He waved at the screen. "So long, losers!"

It was clear that he was not on friendly terms with the other phantoms. But there was no time to think about Thor. My fingers were moving frantically along the keyboard, so fast that my hands were starting to ache.

"When can I stop?" I asked breathlessly. "My hands are getting cramped."

"Stop?" Thor snapped. "That's not allowed. Now, watch out." He pointed to the screen. Siren was darting back and forth, avoiding the big black balls. "Siren doesn't jump high enough." As he spoke, she was knocked over, and I lost a point.

"She's not as agile as I am," Thor commented.

Next came the pendulum swing, in which the gladiator has to hang on a swinging rope while other phantoms try to pull him off. This time I chose Mongo as the gladiator. Thor frowned.

"Never choose Mongo," he told me, pointing to the balding gladiator. "He's got no stamina. Can't hang on for long."

Thor was right. In less than fifteen seconds, the phantoms in black had yanked Mongo down. He fell to the ground with a SPLAT!

Trying to ignore the ache in my fingers, I went on to the Spider's Web. This time I chose Exterminator. He was supposed to cling to the giant net while the other two "spider phantoms" tried to pluck him off.

"He's too slow," Thor said, shaking his head as the phantoms crept up the net quickly. In a second, Exterminator sank down like a lead weight.

"Exterminator is terminated." Thor seemed happy to see the others fail. For him, it proved that no one was as great as he was.

What an ego!

Meanwhile, the dull ache in my fingers had blossomed into pure pain. "I've got to take a break," I pleaded. "Please..."

"Play or pay, Mikey," Thor said, grabbing me by the collar and pulling me out of the chair. "You can stop playing—if you're willing to pay the price."

"I'll pay," I said. "I don't have much money with me, but I have a bank at home."

He laughed and lifted me higher. "Keep your money. You've seen how the curse goes. You've got to pay in pain."

4

The Green Mist

"No!" I kicked and squirmed, but Thor's grip didn't ease. I felt my feet leave the ground and I prepared for the worst.

Instead, I was dropped. I opened my eyes slowly. It was pitch black. I listened for a clue as to what was happening. Silence.

The floor tiles felt cool against my palms as I sat up and looked around, my eyes adjusting. Everything was dark and quiet, but I was still in the computer lab. The electricity had gone out again.

And where Thor had stood, there was now only a thin green mist. His appearance had to be connected to the electrical storm outside.

I crawled over to the computer terminal. My hands were trembling as I reached up and hit the power switch, then popped out the diskette. Thor was shut down, turned off—history! Even if lightning struck again, he couldn't come back if the game wasn't on. Right?

"Mike..." a voice called.

I ducked down quickly. But then I realized it was Mr. Norman. He was standing in the doorway, shining a flashlight into the room.

"You okay?" he asked.

"Sure," I lied.

"Looks like the storm's taken down some power lines," he said. "You ready to head home?"

"Yes, sir!" I shoved my books and disks into my knapsack. On the way out, I picked up the keyboard Thor had knocked onto the floor.

"Is everything shut down in the lab?" asked Mr. Norman. "We wouldn't want our computers booting up in the middle of the night when the power kicks in."

"Everything's off," I said as I followed him out of the room.

I was glad to be out of there—even though I had to ride my bike through a monster of a storm. The fact that I was still shaking didn't help my steering at all on the slick streets.

As I braced myself through a skid, I thought about Thor and the curse. Was it all over? The computer lab had seemed totally empty when Mr. Norman flashed the light through the room.

"Please, let him be gone forever," I said, turning down Baldwin Lane. But as I walked my bike into our garage, I had a feeling that someone was watching me.

"You're soaking wet!" Mom said as I dripped into the kitchen.

What did she expect? "It's pouring."

"Well, take those sneakers off before you go one step further. And dry your hair," she ordered, tossing me a kitchen towel.

I buried my face in the clean, soft towel and took a deep breath. The house felt warm and dry and safe. Maybe I was wrong. Maybe I had seen the last of that phantom from level four.

After dinner, I tried to forget about Thor and do my homework. The chapter I had to read for science class was all about electricity.

As I plodded through the assignment, I thought about those weird sparks Thor had sent flying at me. My chest still hurt when I rubbed it. I rolled up my sweater and...and there was a burn mark! A blistering red line zigzagged across my chest.

"Gross..." I wondered if it would go away. It would be pretty hard to explain once summer came and we peeled down to our trunks to go swimming in the lake.

Still, it was proof that Thor was real. I wasn't

losing my mind. I couldn't wait until the morning to tell Ben. I went out to the hall phone and punched in his number.

"You'll never believe what happened in the computer lab," I said.

I told him everything about the curse, starting with the news that Hacker had fallen off the roof of his house. Finally, I described the weird gladiator who'd popped out of the computer.

"And then he grabbed me by the collar and lifted me into the air—"

"Come on, Mikey," Ben interrupted me. "You're not a very good storyteller."

I bit my lip. Maybe I should have waited to tell him in person. It was an incredibly weird story. But Ben was my best friend. "I'm not making it up, Ben. Really! I even—"

"So I said the Micro-Chip Club is boring," he went on. "Get over it! But don't snow me with a bunch of garbage about a cursed computer game."

There was a click. Then the line went dead. My best friend had hung up on me!

Feeling rotten, I changed into my T-shirt and shorts and climbed into bed. It wasn't the first time Ben and I had argued. I knew he would believe me...eventually. Tomorrow I would show him the burn mark. I rubbed my chest and sighed. It was a crummy end to an awful day.

Even though I was bushed, I didn't sleep well. First, I had a nightmare in which kids I didn't know appeared on my computer screen and warned me, *Don't play the game! It's cursed!*

Flopping over on my back, I dozed off again. This time, I dreamed I was covered with dirt—like the guy in Earth Quest, on level two. Black dirt pressed against me, pushing me deeper and deeper into a grave. I was smothering...choking.

The grave was crushing me to death!

Then the bony hand of a phantom reached up from the dirt and tugged my leg.

I bolted up in bed, shuddering. But when I opened my eyes, I realized that the nightmare wasn't over!

Green smoke pressed against me, robbing me of air. And through the haze, Thor loomed over me!

5

Fried Feathers

"Aaaah!" I rubbed my eyes, hoping he would go away. But when I refocused, the phantom was still there, bigger and meaner than ever. I didn't get it. The thunderstorm was over. So what was he doing here?

"Wake up, weakling!" Thor growled.

I crawled back against the headboard of my bed, pressing into the pillows for cover. But that made him move even closer.

"Scared?" he taunted.

Who wouldn't be? "How did you get here?" I asked weakly. "There's no more thunder and lightning."

"Ha! That storm had nothing to do with my power," he said.

"Then where did you come from?" I asked. "My computer isn't even on now."

"A minor technicality. And it doesn't matter. The point is, I was sick and tired of playing the

29

same game over and over again. And when you entered the Shadow Zone, you gave me a way out, Mikey."

The Shadow Zone? I rubbed my eyes, still groggy. "I don't know anything about a zone. I was just playing a game, that's all."

"Yes," Thor said, "but playing games was becoming your reality. Your mind was between two worlds—and the bridge between the Natural and the Supernatural is the Shadow Zone. Ready to play again?"

"I'm finished with *Phantom Quest.*" As I spoke I was checking the distance to the door, wondering if I could bolt past him. He grunted impatiently.

"I'm not playing that game anymore," I went on. "Never. Ever."

His eyes frosted over. "That's what you think." He pointed at me—but this time I was ready. I wasn't going to get zapped again! I grabbed a pillow and used it as a shield. The sparks flew from his fingertips. A round hole suddenly appeared in the pillowcase. Singed feathers spilled onto the bed. I choked as a foul, burnt smell filled the air.

"Cut it out!" I muttered. "Nobody's going to play anything if you fry me!"

He put his hands on his hips and eyed me as

if I were speaking a foreign language. Then he grabbed me by the foot and gave a tug. I slid across the bed and landed on the floor with a thump. But he didn't stop there. He crossed the room, dragging me along as if I were a sled.

"Where are we going?" I cried.

"To the game." He left me in a heap at the foot of my computer desk. When I sneaked a look at him, Thor was pointing to the monitor. "Play the game," he demanded.

"No way!" My voice came out in a squeak, like a nervous chipmunk. "I mean...I left it on the computer at school."

He reached into my knapsack and pulled out the diskette. I groaned as he held it up, his eyes glowing with blue sparks. "What's this?"

"It's a copy." I sighed. "But the disk is no good. Two of the sectors are—"

"Play the game!" the words rumbled like an earthquake.

I scrambled to my feet and grabbed my glasses from the desktop. In focus, Thor looked ten times worse than he had before.

Then I caught a glimpse of the clock. Three o'clock! I hadn't been up this late since last summer when Ben and I had camped out in his backyard.

I took a deep breath and tried to stall. The

last thing I wanted to do was play this game. If there was a curse on it, I was digging myself in deeper each time I booted up. But how do you say no to a two-ton gladiator?

"Before I play, I have some questions," I said, feeling that strange itchy feeling in my fingers again. Any minute now, they'd have a will of their own. "Are *you* the one who carries out the curse? I mean, did you push Hacker off the roof? And were you the one who sucked Eric down to the bottom of the pool—"

"*Play the game!*" he ordered.

I felt sure that his booming voice would wake my parents. They would come stumbling into my room, bleary-eyed and surprised. Then they'd send Thor zipping back to level four—or at least out of the house.

Until then, I had no choice but to humor the hulk. "I'll play if you answer my questions," I said as I popped in the disk and booted up.

As if I have any choice! I thought as my fingers tapped the keys. Once again, my fingers were on autopilot, driven by Thor. In the battle of wills, I was losing big-time.

"Tell me about the curse," I said as my fingers punched away. "About the other kids."

"They played the bootleg disk," Thor explained, pointing to the blue sea in level one.

"Eric got stuck in level one, so his was a watery grave. We thought he'd drowned, but somehow he got a second life."

"The paramedics resuscitated him," I said aloud, cringing at the evil of the curse. "And the other kids? Hacker...and John's cousin? Are you the one who hurt them?"

"The other phantoms took care of them," he explained. "You're my first solo mission, Mikey. My first time out of the box."

Oh, great! I thought. I've got a rookie monster on my hands!

"Siren took care of the boy in the grave," he explained. "It was a happy coincidence when that bulldozer came along and covered him with dirt."

"Who came up with those awful ways to hurt kids?" I asked.

Thor shrugged. "We had to make the punishment fit the crime. Hacker got caught in level three. But since there were no mountains to climb, Mongo sent him up to his roof. Your friend did well, considering the distance he fell. The other boys were lucky, too. Lucky to be alive."

He smiled at me, his broad face glowing blue in the light from the monitor. "You might not be so lucky, Mikey."

"W-w-w—" I stammered in fear. "What are you planning to do to me?"

"Nothing," he whispered. "Unless you stop playing the game. If and when that happens, we'll have to think up a punishment that matches the level you're on. Level four? A gladiator tournament might be interesting...though I don't think a shrimp like you would do well at all."

My fingers flew over the keys, plugging away at the game in a frenzy. It was 3 A.M., and I was beat. But how was I going to get rid of the gnarly phantom breathing over my shoulder?

Exhausted, I was staring blankly at the computer screen when the door to my bedroom creaked open.

My father stood in the doorway. His brown hair stuck straight up like a rooster's comb. His robe hung crookedly from his shoulders.

"Michael," Dad rasped out in that quiet voice that comes before the storm, "what in the world is going on in here?"

6

Haywire!

"Dad..." Even though I'd sort of gotten hooked on the game, I was relieved to see my father. He would put an end to this awful curse and the hulking phantom who was bullying me around.

But something weird happened when Dad checked out the room. He didn't even flinch. You'd think he was used to seeing a seven-foot giant standing over his son at three in the morning!

"Michael," he added, "I'm waiting for your explanation...."

Curious, I twisted around in my chair. Behind me, there was only thin air. Thor was gone!

"I—I was sleeping when—" I stammered, then stopped dead when I spotted Thor. He'd turned to dust and pressed himself flat against my closet door. Although he looked like a chalk painting, I knew that he could pop back to life in a flash.

"There he is!" I said, pointing at the closet. "He woke me up. He came out of one of my computer games, and he's been driving me nuts, Dad. Would you get rid of him...please?"

"Michael..." Dad scowled. "I'm not in the mood for a joke."

"It's no joke. Really! I need help." My voice cracked as I pleaded.

Dad rested his hand on my forehead, looking worried. "Do you have a fever? Are you feeling nauseous?"

"No. I'm not sick." I pushed his hand away and stared at Thor, plastered against the closet door.

I'm just trying to point out the phantom in my bedroom! I wanted to yell, but it was no use. Dad couldn't save me. He wouldn't even believe Thor existed unless Thor decided to become three-dimensional again.

"Well, it's back to bed now." My father rubbed his eyes, then sighed. "You spend far too much time on that computer, Mike. Your mother is worried about you."

I shut down the computer and flopped down on my bed. "She worries a lot."

"I'm concerned, too," Dad said, shoving the burnt pillow aside to sit next to me. He didn't even notice the burnt, black feathers that were scattered across the spread.

"Computer skills are important," I said. "Nobody ever gives me any credit for what I do best."

"We're proud of your talents," he said evenly. "But a boy your age needs fresh air. Get outside. Play some ball. Ride your bike."

The lecture was familiar. I'd heard it dozens of times before. If only I'd followed it yesterday afternoon....

"For the next two weeks, I'm putting a limit on your computer time," my father announced.

I groaned. "Aw, Dad..."

"No more than two hours a day. That's the law." He headed out, then looked back at Thor. "And *that* is the oddest poster."

"It's out of this world," I muttered.

"Goodnight, Mikey." Dad softly closed the door behind him.

Thor sprang back to life with a deep chuckle. "Where's your brawn, Mikey? Do you always let that gladiator order you around?"

"My name is *Mike*," I said through gritted teeth. "And I have to take orders from him. He's my father."

"Father?" Thor frowned, trying to take this in.

I realized that they didn't have parents or families on level four. "Is that like the game master? The one with the highest score?"

I rolled my eyes. "Sort of. The point is, I have to do what he says."

"We can change that." Thor raised his hands toward the door. "We'll zap Father and—"

"No!" I jumped out of bed and tugged Thor's arms down. "Don't hurt him. You can't go around zapping everyone! Why don't you just go back into level four, where you belong?"

Thor's cold stare sent icicles darting through my blood. "You still don't understand the curse, Mikey." He took off his Viking hat and stuck it onto my head. "You have to play the game. Maybe you should play from the inside. That would be a fitting punishment for your crime. I'll send you to level four."

"Me?" I tugged off the horns, afraid that they'd send me spinning through time and space smack into level four. "How would you do that?"

He flexed his fingers. "One zap. Quick and easy. You won't know what hit you."

I swallowed hard. Would that be so bad? For a long time, I'd lived on the other side of the computer screen. Life was a game, and *Phantom Quest* was the ultimate challenge. But the thought of going into the game was too weird. It seemed so...final. Wasn't it sort of like dying?

"No, thanks," I said, handing him back the horns. "I like it here just fine."

Thor just smiled, and I had an awful feeling he wasn't telling me everything.

I was right.

I didn't get much sleep that night.

First, I had to convince Thor that I'd be better at playing the game with a few hours' rest. But even after he backed off, I felt like a caged prisoner.

I huddled in the corner of the bed, surrounded by a barricade of pillows and blankets that I'd built up to keep Thor at bay.

At one point I was jarred awake by a humming sound and a strange light. A greenish glow. *Thor!* He had unplugged my clock and settled into the corner. His fingers were kind of melted into the electric socket, and he was sucking in power!

The guy actually glowed. His eyes were closed and his wide lips curved in a little smile.

Was that how he got his power—drinking it in when no one was looking? I wondered about it, but I wasn't about to tap him on the shoulder and start asking questions.

The next thing I remember is a banging noise. Someone was knocking on my door.

"Wake up!" my mother called, poking her head in. "It's late. The power went out last night. Our clocks stopped. Better hurry." She popped back out without noticing the muscle-man who glowed beside my computer.

Thor was still plugged in and humming away. Now was my chance. I yanked some clean clothes from a drawer and bolted out the door before he could even blink.

Out in the hall, I ran toward the bathroom.

"Way to hustle, Mikey," Mom called.

By the time I got down to the kitchen, the place looked like a battlefield. Gray smoke hung in the air. Dad had opened the window over the sink and was trying to fan it out with a towel.

"I reset the fuses in the basement, but the toaster's on the fritz," he said.

In the sink were two charred, smoking squares. It looked like a cold cereal morning.

I cracked open the milk container and tipped it over my bowl. A cheesy paste slid out and plopped onto my Cheerios.

"Gross!" I said, gagging at the smell.

"The milk's gone bad," Dad said. "That's strange, though. Even with the electricity out, the refrigerator should keep cold overnight."

As I poured the smelly cereal down the drain, I wondered about the power outage. Maybe the whole area hadn't lost power. The fact that a phantom had been sucking juice from our house's electrical system probably figured into this.

Thor must have made all our appliances go haywire! I wasn't sure how he did it, but these problems clearly had his name written all over them.

Just then, Mom bustled into the kitchen and grabbed two oranges from the fruit bowl. "Did a tornado hit in here?" she asked, cutting the oranges in half and sticking them into the juicer.

That was Thor's best trick.

The minute Mom hit the juicer button, pulp and sticky juice sprayed the room. It splashed over Mom and Dad and me like water from a lawn sprinkler.

Mom let out a shriek. "Eeee!"

"Turn it off!" yelled Dad.

It was definitely going to be a bad day.

7

Bad 'Tudes

It took a while to clean up the mess. Afterward, I went upstairs to wash up. When I sneaked into my room to get a clean sweater and my knapsack, I got a surprise. A good one, at last.

Thor was gone.

He wasn't under the bed. My closet was empty. And he wasn't plastered against the wall.

I wiped my glasses clean and took one more look, but my room was empty. Relieved, I popped the *Phantom Quest* disk out of the computer and wondered if Thor had gone back into the game.

"He must have," I said aloud. And that was where he would stay. As soon as I got to school, I was going to erase the game from the school computer. Then I would destroy this copy, too.

The curse was going to end here.

By the time I got to school, first period had already started. Mom had written me a note. But when I handed it over to Mrs. Wu, the secretary in the office, the principal butted in.

"What's this?" Mr. Borinski said, snapping up the note. "Power out? Where was the power out last night?"

"On Baldwin Lane," I answered. Staring at the principal, I could see why kids called him "the Bear." He was big and burly, with bushy black hair and a stubby beard that covered his face. Even though he kept his hair short, you could see that it was out of control.

He tapped the note against the counter and eyed me suspiciously. "That's surprising. I live in that area and we had no problem."

Well, you didn't have a phantom in your house! I wanted to snap. Instead, I bit my lip. Nobody talked back to Mr. Borinski and lived to tell the tale.

The principal stroked his beard and studied the note. In the end, I guess he decided it wasn't a forgery. "Give him a pass," he told the secretary. "But I suggest that you get to school on time tomorrow, Mr. Willis."

"Yes, sir," I muttered as the Bear fixed his beady eyes on me. It was a look that said *I'll remember you.*

Great! Now I was on the principal's blacklist.

When I got to the computer lab, kids were already tapping away at keyboards. Mr. Norman took my late pass, then explained the assignment. At least *he* didn't give me a hard time.

I scooted into the empty terminal beside Ben, whose eyes were riveted to the screen. Even though he'd hung up on me last night, I wasn't mad anymore. And I wanted to tell him more about the curse and the phantom that had been terrorizing me.

But before I could say a word, Ben burst out, "I have good news...and good news. First, today's assignment is a breeze. And second, I've already finished mine! Time for a little F and G."

"Fun and games? Cool." But as I glanced at the screen, my stomach twisted. It was the lightning bolt logo I knew too well.

"*Phantom Quest*! Ben, don't play that! I told you—it's cursed!"

"Come on, Mikey." Ben grinned, never taking his eyes off the screen. "Curses are bogus. I know you're ticked off 'cause I trashed the Micro-Chips. So I'm sorry. Now, get over it and show me how the game works."

I stared at my best friend, wondering what to do. His face and unblinking eyes seemed mesmerized by the screen. In a minute, he'd be hooked, and it would be all my fault.

I had to act fast. Before Ben could stop me, I reached around the terminal and hit the power switch. The screen blinked, then went black.

"Hey!" Ben slammed his hand down on the desk, then spun around in his chair. "What's your problem?"

"We have to talk," I told him calmly.

"After I play," Ben whined. "Now quit kidding around." He reached for the power switch.

"I'm serious, Ben," I said. "Dead serious. I've never been more serious in my entire life. This isn't like the Ouija board scam or the story about the haunted house on Poploff Hill. There is definitely something weird about this game. And if you value your *fingers*—" I made a chopping motion over his hands "—you'll listen."

Ben's dark eyes went cold for a minute. Then his face came back to life. "Okay," he groaned. "S.E."

"S.E.?" That was a new one to me.

"Start explaining."

Before I could say another word, the tone sounded. "Oh, great," I muttered. "Now I don't have time to erase the game off the hard drive. I wonder if it's safe to leave it till lunch....No one else knows it's there. But there's always some nosy hacker scanning the directory..."

If I didn't want to get in more trouble with

45

Mr. Borinski, I had to get to my second period class.

"I'll explain on the way to gym," I told Ben.

But as soon as we turned into the corridor, I saw him. Taller than any student, brawnier than any teacher, he was impossible to miss in the halls of Woodmont Middle School. What the heck was he doing here?

He was standing at the end of the hall, grinning at me over the bobbing heads of students.

"Oh, no..."

"What? Tell me!" Ben looked from me to Thor, then back again.

"That's him," I whispered, "the phantom."

"The guy who looks like Hulk Hogan...in a cheap suit?"

I nodded. The suit seemed familiar, and as Thor got closer I realized he must have filched it from my father's closet.

The navy necktie with red dancing Santas—a Christmas joke—was slung around his wide neck. The brown pinstripe suit was a bad match. Not to mention the fact that Dad's jacket was stretched tight around Thor's broad shoulders.

"He doesn't look so scary," Ben muttered. "Except for the weird clothes."

"Well, he didn't pop out of your computer and burn you with a lightning bolt."

Ben shrugged. "You got a point there, Mikey. What should we do?"

Tackle him to the floor? Climb on his shoulders and give him a noogie? Report him to Mr. Borinski? None of the options seemed quite right. Especially since I had a feeling that Thor was here for one reason—to get me to play the game.

"Let's ignore him and see what happens," I said, speeding up the pace. As we got closer to the gym, I gave Ben a quick update on the phantom situation. I was telling him about the crazed juicer when we heard the voice.

"Mikey..." Thor's voice boomed down the corridor.

"He's calling you," Ben said, looking back. We ducked into the boys' locker room and pushed past the stragglers.

"Ignore him," I said. "And don't stop here. Let's go straight out to the gym."

"But we have to change," Ben protested. "Coach Rocco will dock our grades again."

It probably sounds weird, but Ben and I were on the verge of flunking gym. It's not that we're wimps. We just don't like to work up a sweat in the middle of the day.

Unfortunately, Mr. Rocco knew how we felt, and he didn't like our attitudes one bit.

"Mister Willis and Mister Huxley," Coach Rocco barked at us. "Care to dress down and join us today?"

I stood my ground. "No, thanks, sir. We'll sit this one out."

Mr. Rocco was not amused. He yanked on the whistle around his neck and marched past a group of students to chew us out.

"There's someone in the locker room we'd rather not run into," Ben explained. I shot him a lethal look. Did he think the coach was giving us points for creativity?

"Well, *excuse* me," Rocco said, dragging out the phrase. That earned a laugh from the other boys. "And just who are you trying to avoid?"

"A big guy named Thor," Ben answered. He turned to me and whispered, "We're in deep, Mikey. Might as well have some fun."

"*Thor?*" The coach winked at the other kids, as if they were all in on a great joke. "God of Thunder?"

"That's the one," Ben said proudly. "He's actually a gladiator from level four of—"

The shrill sound of Coach Rocco's whistle cut Ben off. At the same time, I noticed the locker room door fly open. Thor emerged, his heavy footsteps pounding on the wood floor.

"That's enough, Huxley," the coach snapped.

"And you too, Willis. Your attitudes stink—and it's going to be reflected in your grades. I've told you time and again that..."

The coach's lecture dragged on while I watched Thor walking around the gym as if he owned the place. He checked out the kids one by one. Then he paused beside Mr. Rocco as the lecture heated up.

"You will not talk," the coach barked. "You will not laugh. You will not even breathe in my class! Do you understand?"

Ben and I nodded.

The coach turned and saw Thor. "What are *you* doing in my class?" he bellowed.

"I've come to play the game," Thor told him.

I was getting pretty sick of those words.

"What?" Mr. Rocco did a double take, then said, "You're in the wrong place, pal."

"Not me," Thor said. He pointed at the coach and before the coach could say a word, a stream of sparks shot out from Thor's fingertips. The blinding bolt hit Mr. Rocco in the chest.

Shouts and shrieks filled the gymnasium. "Not again," I said, jumping to my feet.

Ben grabbed my arm. "Stay back!"

When Thor lowered his hand, the only thing left of Coach Rocco was the silver whistle on the gym floor.

8

Vanished

"Unbelievable!" Ben's mouth hung open.

"What did you do to him?" I ran down the bleachers and jumped to the floor at Thor's feet.

"It's a trick!" Devon O'Dell called out. "Coach Rocco's pulling a fast one on us."

"So where is he?" someone else shouted.

"I got rid of him." Thor picked up the coach's whistle and looked at it curiously. "He had a bad attitude."

I wanted to knock on Thor's brain and ask, "Anybody in there?" But then again, there was a good chance that no one would answer.

"I told you, you can't just go around zapping people." I pulled Thor away from the other kids, who were combing the area looking for clues. Devon had them convinced that it was a trick and that the coach was going to pop out from behind the bleachers.

"Now the whole class has seen you," I told

Thor. "You've got to bring the coach back....Or is it too late?"

"Is he *dead*?" Ben's eyes flashed as he looked from me to Thor.

"Loosen up, Mikey," Thor said. "This wouldn't have happened if you hadn't slipped out of the house this morning. Don't you know you can't get away from a curse?"

"No kidding. Were the haywire juicer and toaster part of the curse, too?"

"I was just having a little fun." Thor grinned happily. "I think I'm getting the hang of this world. See?" He lifted his tie. "I even borrowed some of Father's clothes so no one would realize I came from level four." He looked at the other kids in shorts, T-shirts, and tank tops. "But I see that *some* people dress like me."

"They're wearing *gym* clothes," I explained. "Shorts are okay when you're working out."

"Good." Thor peeled off the shirt and tie as he talked. "I'm getting into this reality thing, Mikey. Pretty soon, I'll be a pro."

"Great," I said sarcastically. "Now could you tell us what happened to our coach?" I had a bad feeling. Last night, Thor had mentioned zapping me into the game. *Quick and easy*, he'd said last night. "Did you send Coach Rocco into the game?" I whispered.

51

"Good one!" Thor clapped me on the back. "You're onto my strategy. Ready to join him?"

"What's he talking about?" Ben asked me.

But there was no time to explain. I didn't want to get zapped into the *Phantom Quest* game. The more I thought about it, the scarier it seemed. But if I said yes, it might give me the break I needed. "Sure," I lied. "As soon as I learn a few more tricks of the game. We'll hit the computer lab at lunchtime."

"*Hit* the lab?" Thor asked.

"We'll meet you there," I said.

"Got it." Thor had stripped down to his shorts and shiny tank top. The class started to scatter, but Thor blew the whistle and smiled. "Who's for a round of Spider's Web?"

It didn't take long for our gym class to warm up to Thor.

"This guy's a maniac," Ben muttered as we collapsed on the sidelines. "I'm sorry I didn't believe you last night, Mikey. It just sounded so...so *weird*. But I should have given you the benefit of the doubt."

"That's okay." I lifted my glasses to wipe the sweat from around my eyes. Thor had insisted that Ben and I change into our gym clothes and participate. In the locker room, I'd shown Ben the burn mark on my chest. I think that had scared him as much as seeing our coach zapped into oblivion...or wherever it was he had gone.

The whistle blew, and Thor clapped his hands at us. "Come on, you two! Get the lead out." He nudged my shoulder playfully. "These matches are a lot more fun in reality."

After a few rounds of Spider's Web and bowling, which we played with the school's giant cage ball, everyone seemed to have forgotten about Mr. Rocco. Even Devon O'Dell had only mentioned him once or twice, but what do you expect from the class suck-up?

When the tone sounded, Ben and I were relieved. It was our chance to get away from Thor—at least until lunchtime.

In the back of my mind, I hoped that one of the teachers would snag him before then. Maybe they'd call the police—or the National Guard! They would have tanks and helicopters and squawking megaphones. "We've got you surrounded, phantom! Surrender!"

Ben nudged me. "Snap out of it, Mikey." We were sitting at a table in the library, supposedly writing a report on Thomas Jefferson. Instead, we were chewing our pencils and trying to figure out what to do about Thor.

"Somebody's bound to catch him," Ben said,

scratching his head. "You can't get anything past Mr. Borinski. Besides, people are going to notice that Coach Rocco is missing. You don't just zap a gym teacher and get away with it."

I rested my chin in my hands. "I don't know. So far, Thor hasn't been caught. Look at what happened with the kids in gym. They all thought he was a cool substitute who knows how to do amazing magic tricks. I swear that guy could get away with murder."

"You don't think—" Ben's dark eyes flashed. "Is Coach Rocco D.M.?"

"Dead meat?" I shrugged off the chill that shuddered through my body. "The only thing I know for sure is that my copy of *Phantom Quest* has a curse on it. And Thor is here to carry it out. But if we can convince him to go back into the game...maybe it'll all be over."

"Is that why we're meeting him in the computer lab?" Ben asked.

I nodded. "The only problem is, he thinks that *I'm* going into the game."

"What?" Ben dropped his pencil. "No way!"

"Way."

"You can't do it," Ben insisted. "You aren't going to do it...are you?"

I let out a deep sigh. Just yesterday, the thought of playing *Phantom Quest* twenty-four hours a day thrilled me. But now it gave me the creeps. Imagine having to dodge giant bowling balls or fight off phantoms without a single break! The game would get boring fast.

"I don't want to go," I told Ben. "But I may have to fake it until we can trick Thor into going back."

Ben frowned. "This plan gives me the willies. How can you trick the master of the game?"

Of course, *my* luck didn't change, and neither did Thor's. He made it through two more periods of gym with glowing reviews. By the time Ben and I met him in the computer lab, we were on edge.

"Ready to go?" Thor asked, pushing my chair to the computer terminal.

"What if he wants to come back?" Ben asked Thor, putting a hand on my shoulder as if he could hold me in this dimension. "What if Mike gets sick of the game?"

"Not Mikey," Thor said. "He lives for the game. That's why he entered the Shadow Zone."

Trying to control my fear, I worked the keyboard frantically. Ben and I had rehearsed our plan. He was going to stall, while I played through the program, looking for a back door.

When a program is designed, sometimes the

creator adds a feature like a password or back door. It's a trick that can let you get out of the program, or maybe take a shortcut. That was what I was looking for...a trick that might suck Thor back into the computer.

Okay, so it was a lame plan. But what else could we do?

Ben's mouth dropped open in amazement as I whizzed through level one, then began Earth Quest. "You're really good at this game."

"It's not me," I admitted. "It's the curse."

"Mikey has to play the game," Thor explained, "whether he wants to or not. That's his curse."

"So tell me," Ben said, cracking his knuckles nervously. "How many levels are in this game?"

"Five," Thor answered.

I hadn't realized I was close to conquering the whole game. "What's level five like?"

"It's called 'Final Quest,'" Thor explained. "But I've never been there."

"'Final Quest,'" Ben said. "Sounds...final. So what about the other levels? Have you been there?"

"All gladiators train on the lower levels," Thor explained. "If you look closely at the phantoms, you may recognize us. But in the first three levels we're covered in black. We're not allowed to unmask until level four."

"Pretty creepy," Ben said. "So how long have you been a gladiator?"

"Since the program was created," Thor answered. "What's with all the questions? Are you ready to go? Or do you want to keep playing the game till the day you die?"

"I—We—" I stammered.

"He's looking for a way to get rid of *you*, meathead!" Ben burst out. "Don't you see? If you just go back into the computer, everything will be okay again. We'll destroy the bootleg disk. The curse will end, and our lives will be normal again. So why don't you go back into the game?"

Thor looked surprised. "But I *like* reality," he said. "I was getting bored on level four. I don't want to go home. I'm here to stay, guys."

Just then, a popping sound came out of the computer. I rolled my chair back as the monitor exploded in a burst of green smoke.

"Not again!" I groaned. The air rumbled as I tugged Ben under a desk for cover.

The green smoke seemed to scare even Thor. He backed away, gasping for air.

Huddled together, Ben and I watched as the smoke swirled into the shape of a sword. Then it separated into three shapeless blobs.

"What is it?" Ben asked. "Tell me!"

But before I could answer, the three blobs

formed distinctive shapes. There was a very muscular woman with a vicious smile. A rubbery man with round eyes that seemed to pop out of his mostly bald head. And a man with features so square he could have been a steel robot.

Siren, Mongo, and Exterminator.

The other three gladiators were coming to this side of the screen!

9

Trouble Times Four

Ben grabbed my arm. "Who are *they*?"

"The other gladiators from level four," I said as the phantom gladiators came into focus.

A second later, they sprang to life...and fell to the ground in a heap. The giant mound of beefy biceps and muscular legs was like a pileup at Wrestlemania.

"Get off of me!" Siren snapped.

"I can't help it," Mongo whined, rolling away from the others. "It's not every day that I get booted out of the screen."

Exterminator sprang to his feet. "Stop your complaining and get ready to fight," he said, checking out the room. "This is going to be a very satisfying mission."

"Vengeance, at last." With a wicked smile, Siren leaped to her feet and spun toward Thor. She had to be seven feet tall! But then again, they all seemed to be about seven feet tall.

"We've come to cream *you*!" Siren poked a long, pointed nail at Thor. "No one is allowed to stay in reality. You were planning to break the rules, and that's forbidden."

Thor flicked her hand away with a growl. "I'm quaking in my boots," he said sarcastically, but I could see he was a little shaken by the arrival of the other three phantoms.

"You've gotten too comfortable in reality," said Mongo, the bald one. "You're about to blow your first mission."

"So we're going to keep you in line," Siren added, licking her red lips.

"Ha!" Thor scowled. "I can beat any one of you at any time. I've always outscored you in the game. What makes you think you have any power over me at all?" he demanded, folding his arms.

"We have a new strategy," Exterminator said. "We've formed a team."

"Team?" Confused, Thor looked down at me. "Is that a secret weapon?"

I shook my head. "That's when people work together," I explained. "It'll be three of them against one of you. Not really fair..." I hesitated when Siren leaned down to give Ben and me an evil glower.

"Are these boys your prey?" Siren asked, kicking back the desk to get a better look at us. "I recognize this one," she said, pointing at me. "He's toyed with me endlessly."

"He can't help it," Ben blurted. "It's the curse—"

"It didn't begin with the curse," Exterminator interrupted. "This boy was obsessed. He made us jump, swing, run, tumble.... I'm so sick of being manipulated by kids like you," he told me. "It's time for revenge. Now it's *our* turn to play with *you*."

Mongo's hairless forehead wrinkled as he snorted at us. "Thin, scrawny things." He leaned down close, and his round, goggled eyes gave me the creeps. "How about a little round of Spider's Web?" he asked, flicking his tongue like a snake.

"No way," Ben snapped, crawling out to face the phantoms. "You can't just come here and take your frustrations out on innocent people."

"Oh, yeah?" Siren smiled. "Just watch us."

She pointed a dark red fingernail at Ben. Red sparks shot out of her fingertips. But before they hit, they were intercepted by a jolt of lightning from Thor! He zapped Siren's rays and sent them skittering off to the side.

When the air cleared, Ben was left blinking at the two angry gladiators.

"How dare you cross me!" Siren sneered at Thor.

He put his hands on his hips. "The kid's on my team."

I looked at Thor suspiciously. Not bad for a guy who didn't even know what a team was two minutes ago. Was he actually defending us?

"Your team?" Mongo snapped. "Explain."

"For the tournament I planned for Mikey," Thor said, and I could see that he was making things up as he went along. "Since his punishment must fit level four, I was going to put him through a grueling tournament. Just like in the game."

"Clever," Siren agreed.

"I take it this child will be in it, too," Mongo said, leering at Ben.

"Wait a minute!" Ben held up his hands. "I never played *Phantom Quest*."

"You started to," Exterminator said, wagging his finger at Ben. "We saw you. You're as good as cursed."

"No!" I shouted. It wasn't fair to drag Ben into this.

"Both boys will play in the tournament," Thor said, and that seemed to end the argument.

"Fine," said Siren. "We'll have the tournament today. How about four o'clock reality time?"

"You're on," Thor said, nodding.

"In the meantime, we'll find some bigger kids to toy with," Exterminator said as he glanced out the door. "It's time to get back at the kids who kept me scrambling around in level four."

Mongo glared at us one last time, then followed the other gladiators out of the lab. Thor folded his arms and frowned.

"Can't you stop them?" Ben asked him. "Zap them back into the computer or something."

Thor frowned. "Gladiators cannot zap each other. Our powers cancel each other out."

"But you just zapped that red ray," I said.

"I deflected it," Thor explained. "That's different."

"Why don't you all go back into the computer and leave our school the way it was?" Ben pleaded.

"It's too late to back out," Thor said. "The tournament is on. Now you must play." Thor's broad face was pale. The appearance of the other phantoms had really thrown him.

"If we beat the other gladiators," Thor continued, "there's no way they can make me return to level four."

"Then we'll have to beat them," Ben said.

"Yeah, right." I flexed my skinny arm. "We'll cream 'em."

"At least we got the big guy." Ben pointed to Thor, who actually beamed.

"Do you think they'll hurt anyone?" I asked as the towering figures disappeared at the other end of the hall.

"They'll mow down anyone who stands in their way," said Thor evenly.

"No way they'll get past Mr. Borinski," Ben said smugly. "The Bear will have them crying for their mommies before the day is over."

Thor turned to me and asked, "What's a mommy?"

Ben was wrong. The three evil phantoms had not only made it past the principal, they had zapped Mr. Borinski into oblivion.

Or at least that was the word around school. I didn't see it myself, but I'd seen enough to know that the rumor was probably a fact.

Of course, the one being blamed for this whole mess was me. John Miluski told everyone I'd been messing around with a bootleg copy of *Phantom Quest*, and kids had heard that the game was cursed. Now everyone seemed to think that I'd brought the curse down on our school.

With all the stories buzzing the halls, everyone was pretty tense. By the time we sat down in math class, I felt like I was swimming through a nightmare. Everywhere I looked, I saw wide eyes, hunching shoulders, and pale faces. The kids of Woodmont Middle School were scared out of their wits.

Even Mrs. Fernandez looked a little pasty as she told us to open our textbooks to page eighty-seven. Then she asked Vickie Goldberg to write the first homework problem on the board.

Vickie went up to the board. She was drawing curvy numbers when the door banged open, making me jump.

It was Siren, and from the way she fanned her pointed nails through the air, she seemed to be out for blood. She checked out the room until her eyes locked on Vickie.

No, not Vickie! My heart hammered. She was a cute girl who always had something nice to say.

Siren picked up a piece of chalk, scraped it on the board, and smiled. "This will come in handy. We'll keep score at the tournament."

A few kids snickered, but most of us were deadly silent. Everyone had heard the rumors of the curse and the phantoms stalking our school, happily zapping away at anyone who dared to challenge them.

As soon as she saw the giant woman dressed

in a red leotard, Vickie dropped the chalk and backed away. But Mrs. Fernandez was not amused.

"Just a moment, miss," she said briskly. "This classroom is a place of learning, not fun and games."

Siren blew chalk dust off her fingertips, then pointed at Mrs. Fernandez. "Okay, teach, here's your first lesson. Never mess with a phantom."

In a flash, my math teacher was subtracted from reality.

10

No More Pencils, No More Books

Most of the kids managed to smother their whimpers, but a few shrieks slipped out from the back of the room, where Devon O'Dell was having a panic attack.

"I love doing that!" Siren took a deep breath. Then she gathered up all the chalk and swept out of the classroom.

"What's going on?" Vickie Goldberg asked, her hands quivering as she covered her mouth.

"Mrs. Fernandez has been zapped," said John Miluski. "And she's not the first. I heard it happened to two other teachers."

"Looks like we won't have any math homework tonight," Tony Benedetti said, closing his book.

I buried my face in my hands, feeling awful. Was it just yesterday that I'd wished that I could zap Mrs. F and turn her into space dust? Things had changed pretty fast. At the moment, I would have given anything for a normal, boring math class with long problems and tons of homework.

A hand touched my shoulder. "Come on, Mikey," said Ben. "I think I know a way out of this mess."

I grabbed my knapsack and followed Ben out of the classroom. Sure, I felt a little guilty bailing out of math class before it was over, but who was going to stop me?

"Okay, Benarooski," I said as we walked along. "What's the plan?"

"We've got to come clean with Mr. Norman," Ben said. "You have to tell him that you copied *Phantom Quest* onto the school's computer."

I swallowed. "Great. So I get a one-way pass to detention. Then what?"

"Then maybe he can help us figure out how to get rid of the phantoms and destroy the program," said Ben. "Mr. Norman is the *ultimate* computer buff. Better than Hacker. Even better than you."

"More experienced," I corrected him.

"Whatever. The point is, if there's a back door—a password or something—Mr. Norman will know how to find it."

"I should have thought of that," I muttered.

Ben smiled. "That's why you hang with me, Mikey," he said, "for the O.S.G."

"Translation."

"Occasional stroke of genius," Ben explained.

We flung open the door to the computer lab and barreled inside. But Mr. Norman wasn't sitting at his desk. He wasn't puttering around at the terminals or adjusting the window shades to keep the sun off the computers.

"Where's Mr. Norman?" I asked Lori Waters, who was playing Super Sleuths on the computer. The monitor made her pale blond hair glow green.

She shrugged. "Don't know. He didn't show up for class."

"Didn't show up?" Ben and I said at the same time. Something was very wrong. Mr. Norman was super-reliable, like a precision clock.

"Maybe he went to the office," Ben suggested.

"When a class was scheduled?" I shook my head.

"Think he was zapped?" Ben asked softly so that none of the other kids could hear. "Or do you think he heard the rumors and headed for home?"

"I don't know." I sighed, then headed over to a free terminal. "But we might as well check out the game. We can keep looking for a back door."

I didn't want to admit that I felt that strange itchy feeling in my fingers—the curse. I had to play *Phantom Quest*. I couldn't help it.

While Ben paced nervously, I pounded the keyboard. I played my way through the first three levels, trying different ways to get out of the program. The game was getting harder; the number of phantoms had multiplied.

"Nothing is working," I muttered.

"Mr. Norman will be back any minute," Ben said hopefully. "He'll help us."

I cleaned my glasses and tried again. This time, I focused on getting to level four. When I got there, I couldn't believe my eyes.

"Um, Ben. You'd better have a look at this."

"What is it?" Ben asked.

Then he saw the monitor.

Choose your gladiator. That was the command. But these gladiators were eerily familiar.

Coach Rocco was in one box. Mr. Borinski stared out from another square. Mrs. Fernandez was there, looking dazed. And in the bottom right-hand corner was the face of Mr. Norman, looking like a yellow marshmallow man.

"Oh, no..." Ben gasped.

They were trapped inside level four.

11

Horror Show

It was a horror show of Woodmont teachers.

"I can't play anymore." Feeling sick, I pushed my chair away. Believe it or not, I didn't want to see my teachers sweating it out on level four.

"You have to!" said Ben. "Otherwise, we'll never find the password." He rolled my chair right back to the computer.

Ben was right. With a sigh, I continued to play. I chose Mrs. Fernandez, and she was surprisingly good at dodging the giant bowling ball. "I didn't know she was so athletic," I said.

"See!" Ben patted me on the back. "It's not that bad."

Hoping for inspiration from the ultimate computer guru of all times, I chose Mr. Norman for the next round. It was a bad choice. He was so out of shape that he could barely hang on to the spider's web. Once the phantom spiders gave him a tug or two, he was a goner.

"Bummer," Ben said. "Want to try again? The Bear looks pretty strong."

"I'll keep trying," I said, feeling discouraged. I was working with the Bear when Ben called me to the window.

"Quick," he said, motioning me over. "There's trouble."

I joined Ben and the two other kids from our class who were looking out at the schoolyard. "What's going on?" I asked.

"The phantoms are practicing for the tournament," Ben explained.

We watched as Exterminator scaled the flagpole. Groups of kids stood around the schoolyard watching too. A few kids cheered loudly when Exterminator reached the metal ball at the top. Then he slid back down, landing just a few feet from Stephanie Mayhews.

Her red curls bobbed as she wagged a finger at him. She was class president, and she loved to boss people around. I cringed. She was probably telling the phantom to stay off school property.

Exterminator listened to her for a second. Then it was all over. With a grin, he raised his hands and zapped her with an orange ray. Stephanie Mayhews was gone.

I groaned.

"Did you see that?" Lori gasped.

"Now they're zapping kids!" Christopher Leonard gulped.

"It's awful," Lori said, nervously scraping back her blond bangs. "They don't care who they hurt. Why did you bring them here, Mike?"

"I didn't!" I protested, taking in the frightened faces around me. "I mean, I didn't do it on purpose. It was an accident. Sort of."

No one seemed to buy my story.

"Hey," Ben said smoothly. "Ease off. Mike and I have the situation under control. Those phantoms outside won't last long." He grinned and added, "They're made of *dust!*"

Ben to the rescue. He could talk a good game, and everyone seemed to buy it for the moment. But I knew the truth. I'd unleashed a team of monsters on my school, and I had no idea how to stop them.

I was leaning on the windowsill, trying to ignore the queasy feeling in my stomach, when Vickie Goldberg came in. "I've been looking all over for you two," she said. "That big blond guy in the gym wants to see you."

Ben and I looked at each other and nodded.

"He's weird," Vickie added, squinting at me. "Is he really a substitute? 'Cause he dresses just like those three phantoms."

"He's trouble," Ben said, squeezing her elbow

as he went by. "Stay away from him."

If only we could do the same.

We found Thor doing push-ups in the center of the gym. "Sixty-three...sixty-four..." he counted, pumping away. The guy hadn't even broken a sweat.

"Your friends are going wild," I reported. Watching Thor spring to his feet, I realized I wasn't so scared of him anymore. Compared to the other three phantoms, he was a pussycat. "They're zapping everybody. Teachers...kids. They even terminated our principal!"

"They are no friends of mine," Thor said, springing to his feet. "I've fought them all my life on level four. That's why we've got to win this tournament. I don't intend to go back into the computer and spend eternity competing with those morons."

"Reality check!" I said. "There's no way we're going to win the tournament! Those phantoms are going to put Ben and me in the hospital. Then they're going to send you packing back to level four."

"It's true," Ben admitted. "We can't beat those beefy phantoms. Even with you, Thor. Isn't there some other game we can challenge them to play?"

"You're forgetting the curse," Thor said. "This tournament is your punishment."

"Can't you forget the curse for a minute?" said Ben. "We'll make a deal with you, Thor. You help us out of this jam, and we'll try to help you...uhm...adjust to reality."

Ben gave me a hopeful look and I rolled my eyes. Why don't you just promise the guy the moon! I thought.

But the plan seemed to cheer Thor up. "That sounds like a good deal. But I don't know what will happen to me if I don't carry out the curse."

"We'll worry about that later," Ben said, clapping him on the back. "Shake on it?"

Thor stared at his outstretched hand, then shook it. "It's a deal."

We had one strong ally. Now we just had to worry about these other crazed phantoms. "So the tournament is out," I said. "We just need to think of a way to corner the phantoms using our brains instead of brawn."

"They're not going to be happy about canceling the tournament," Ben pointed out. "They've been practicing all afternoon."

I shoved my hands into my jeans' pockets and shrugged. "So...who says we're going to tell them?"

"G.I.! Great idea!" Ben snapped his fingers. "We'll be a no-show."

"No-show?" Thor looked confused.

"Just follow us," Ben said. "We'll take care of everything."

12

On the Run

It wasn't hard to sneak away from the school unnoticed. Our school is shaped like a U, and the schoolyard is in the center. So the other phantoms couldn't see us as we crept out the front door and cut down a wooded street across from the school.

Once we were a safe distance away, there was the question of what to do with Thor. Dressed in tight shorts and a red tank top with a lightning bolt on the front, the guy attracted a lot of attention. Even though he'd left his Viking hat at home, he was still seven feet tall and built like Arnold Schwarzenegger.

Besides, we had to keep a low profile. As we walked through Woodmont, I kept looking back over my shoulder, afraid that the three phantoms might be trailing us.

It was already quarter to four. In fifteen minutes, they would probably figure out that we'd bailed. I wanted to be hidden away when they came looking for us.

We cut across the parking lot of the shopping center, hoping to hide out at Aldo's Pizza Place. There were two video games in the back with my initials in the top three spots. But we didn't get that far.

"Are you the super hero from the Z-Man Comics?" some kid asked Thor.

"Oh, do you want his autograph, dear?" the kid's mother asked. She fished a pen out of her purse and handed it to Thor.

Thor held the pen up to the sun to examine it. The guy didn't have a clue what to do with it. That's what happens when you spend the whole day in gym class.

"Sign the kid's notebook," I muttered under my breath.

"Sign?"

Ben and I looked at each other. Thor didn't know how to write! I guess literacy wasn't important on level four.

"Rub the tip of the pen against the page," I whispered.

With a shrug, Thor followed my instructions. When he finished, the kid took the notebook and stared at the scrawl. "Bozgoop?" He wrinkled his nose. "Is that you?"

"That's right," Ben said smoothly. "You got Bozgoop's autograph, you lucky dog."

By that time, a small crowd of shoppers had gathered, and everyone wanted a piece of the action. The little kids loved Thor. I even saw some older people looking on, like Mrs. Gantry, our next-door neighbor.

"One at a time," Ben shouted, organizing the mob. "Don't push. There's plenty of Bozgoop to go around."

A lanky teenager got Thor to sign the sleeve of his T-shirt, then complained, "Hey, he signed mine 'Zagmeep.' Is this guy for real, or what?"

Ben patted Thor's beefy biceps and smiled. "Believe me, he's the real deal."

As usual, Thor seemed to be enjoying all the attention. He tousled the hair on one kid's head and gave a group of mothers a little wink. I had to admit, he was adept at learning new games. But all this attention was making me nervous. Especially when I noticed the color on Thor's T-shirt change. It was pale. And his beefy hands seemed to waver, like those heat waves you see floating over a hot street in the summer.

Thor was beginning to fade.

"Well, gang," I said, "it's time for this super hero to move on."

Ben got my drift immediately. "He needs to

right wrongs. Stop crime. Keep Woodmont safe for all you good citizens." Ben could really lay it on thick.

We hustled Thor away from the cheering crowd and made a bee-line away from the shopping center.

"What's the matter with you?" I asked Thor. "You're turning to dust."

"I'm losing power," he said, holding up his hands, which were a blur of buzzing molecules. "Need juice."

"Juice?" Ben asked. "What's he talking about?"

"Electricity," I said quickly. "He needs energy. Where can we go?"

Neither of us wanted to take Thor home unless it was absolutely necessary. Ben's mom didn't work, so we knew she'd greet us with a million questions. And I had a feeling my parents still hadn't gotten over the way Thor had turned our appliances into an electrical circus. But I knew that we had to get out of the open. As it was, we were easy prey for Siren, Mongo, and Exterminator.

"We need a quiet place," Ben said. "A place where we won't run into a bunch of nosy kids."

After a moment we both said: "The library!"

It was only three blocks away. Thor had to

duck to get through the old wooden doorway, but after that we were home free.

Except, of course, for the blue-haired old lady that worked the front desk.

"You, young man!" She pointed to Thor. "Haven't I seen you on that T.V. show, *Amazing Gladiators*?"

"I *am* a gladiator!" Thor beamed, leaning up against the counter. At last, someone seemed to speak his language. "Would you like my autograph?" he offered.

"Later," Ben insisted, tugging him toward the back room. "We have some important...uh, research to do."

We found a deserted table in the corner, where we tried to look casually around for an electrical outlet. But we were all restless. We couldn't talk without getting shushed by the librarian, and we weren't in the mood to do heavy reading. Besides, Thor could only look at the pictures.

Finally, Thor got up from the table and went over to the bookcase against the wall.

"What's he doing?" Ben whispered. "Picking out another book?"

We went over and found Thor combing the bare wall at the edge of the bookcase. "This will work just fine," he said, squatting down so that he was level with the wall outlet.

Then he stuck his fingers in.

"Yikes!" Ben gasped, jumping back.

A humming sound rang out as Thor lit up like a Christmas tree. He smiled and closed his eyes.

Amazed, Ben nudged me. "He's...he's plugged himself in!"

13

Plugged In!

I nodded, standing clear of the glow. "That's what he did last night, too. That's the way he regenerates."

"Too weird," Ben said.

After a minute or so, the lights went out. I guess Thor had sucked too much from the old building's electrical system.

Soon, the librarian was calling through the shadowy stacks. "Attention, please! I'm afraid we'll have to close the library. Our fuses are blown and we can't reset them."

Thor sprang to his feet and stretched. "That's better."

"Did you have to suck the juice out of the *whole* building?" I muttered under my breath.

"What now?" Ben asked. "We're running out of places to hide."

"I guess we'll have to go to my house," I said reluctantly. Then I turned to Thor. "But you have to promise to stay away from the electrical sockets."

Blue light glimmered from his eyes, casting shadows in the dark library. "I've got enough power to tide me over for a while," he said.

"Well, I could use a Q.E.S. myself," said Ben. When I gave him a look, he added, "Quick energy snack."

The light from the refrigerator hit Ben's face as he leaned inside. "Hey, Mikey. Looks like someone emptied out your fridge."

"We had to toss a lot of stuff out this morning," I said, reminding him about how Thor had played with the house's electrical system.

"Wow." Ben took a seat at the kitchen table and opened a pack of Oreos. He waved a cookie at Thor. "You've been causing a lot of trouble."

Thor shrugged. "It was just a trick."

"Well, think of a trick to outsmart the phantoms," I said as I poured us each a glass of juice. "We've got to figure out a way to get those three phantoms back into the computer—and get everyone else back out alive."

"If I return to the game, the coach will reappear in reality," Thor explained. "But I have no control over the others who are trapped. No one can come back to reality until the phantom who zapped them goes back into the game."

"How are we going to talk those three goons into going back?" Ben asked. "They've taken over our school."

"And they're zapping their way through the kids in our class." I rubbed my chest as I thought about the problem. The burn mark had started to fade, but it itched like crazy.

Ben poured himself another glass of apple juice, then slammed the jug on the table. "I got a question, Thor. You know how you need to charge yourself up with electricity?" Thor nodded. "Well, what about the other phantoms? Don't they run out of energy, too?"

"Of course," Thor answered. "We were born of megawatts. Without electric power, we fade."

"That's it!" Ben's eyes had that wild look. "We cut off their power."

"Hold on," I said. "Are you planning to black out the entire state of Illinois—or just this county?"

"We can start with the town," Ben suggested.

I bit my lip. "That would stop them for a while. But eventually the power would be restored—along with the phantoms. It's still not a solution."

"Well, I'm running out of ideas," Ben admitted. "And we're running out of time. What if the phantoms catch up with us tonight? What if they're waiting for me when I get home?"

"That's unlikely," Thor said.

"What?" Ben and I asked at once.

"The phantoms won't be able to visit you at home—unless you live very near the school. They can't travel too far from the program without losing power."

"Really?" Ben was relieved. Then he frowned. "Hey, why didn't you tell us before?"

"And if that's true, how come you're here?" I said. "Don't you have to stay near the school computer?"

Thor reached into my knapsack. "I've got this," he said, holding up a diskette. It was the *Phantom Quest* disk I'd gotten from Hacker.

I felt like a light bulb had switched on over my head. "Whoa! You're still attached to the game?" When Thor nodded, I went on, "So if I erase the copies of the game from the disk and from the school computer, you and the other three phantoms will disappear!"

"Well..." Thor seemed upset. "Probably. But that would also wipe *me* out."

Ben pressed my arm. "And if you erase the programs, you'll wipe out the people who were sucked inside."

Ben was right.

I leaned my chair back so that I could make eye contact with Thor. "Look, it's not that I want to get rid of you. But those other three phantoms have to go. And you've got to admit that you don't exactly fit in around here."

Thor twisted an Oreo open. "You're right. Reality isn't the place for me. But I don't want to go back to level four. It's boring. There's got to be someplace that's more challenging. A place where I belong."

I could relate. I knew how it felt to be an odd duck in the pond. Last year, I'd been too small to try out for any of the school teams. So I'd started spending more time at the computer, learning every game inside out.

Since then, I'd grown a little. And somehow, Ben and I had avoided the dweeb pit. We'd eked out reputations as normal guys who happened to be computer whiz kids. We had a niche.

But how do you find a place for a guy like Thor? WANTED: Home for seven-foot gladiator with an appetite for electricity!

"Tell us about the game," I said, waving a cookie at Thor. "Do you know anything about a back door in the program—a password put in by the game designer?"

He scratched his head. "I never heard of a password on level four. But the designer..." He closed his eyes, trying to remember. "He must be the one who started the curse. Ever since I was a rookie phantom, I remember the order: players who use an illegal copy of the disk must be punished."

I blinked. "So maybe the curse *is* just a virus that the designer put into the program."

My heart started to beat faster. At last, a clue! "We've got to get some details from the company that makes the game. Most of those places have 800-numbers you can call."

"Are you kidding?" Ben shook his head. "We have a bootleg copy. They'll laugh in our faces."

"We don't have to tell them that." I pulled out the phone book and looked up the number of Woodmont's biggest computer store. The clerk who answered the phone told me that *Phantom Quest* was manufactured by a company called Shadow Zone, Inc., and he gave me their number.

"This is so weird!" I told Ben and Thor. "Get this! The company is called Shadow Zone. Their number is 1-800-THE-ZONE!"

"Creepy!" Ben shuddered.

Thor's eyes sparked with fear. "That's the Creator. Don't tell him I'm here."

"Don't worry," I said, punching in the number. "I can handle this."

Ben picked up the living room extension to listen in. From my perch on the kitchen counter, I could see Thor huddled by the receiver next to him.

The line rang twice, then a woman's nasal voice answered, "Shadow Zone."

I told her that I'd bought the game recently and was having trouble with some of the phantoms on level four. "My question is, can you tell me if there's a back door? Something that'll reset the program when the phantoms...uh...go haywire?"

"I can't give out that information," she said. "Don't you want to be challenged by the game?"

"Believe me, it's been challenging," I said. "But I'm really jammed up here."

"Well, maybe I can help you," she said. "What's the serial number of your software?"

I gulped. I'd forgotten that each game the company sold had a number used for tracking. "You know," I lied, "I lost the box my disk came in."

"The number is stamped on the disk."

Not on mine! I thought.

Ben was giving me the signal to hang up, but I'd come so close. "Please," I begged. "Can't you help me? If the designer put in a back door, what level do you think it would be on?"

Silence. Then she sighed. "Level five is the Creator's favorite," she said. "It's the only level with a heart."

"Will I find the back door there?" I asked.

"Kid, if your disk doesn't have a serial number, it's a bootleg," she said firmly. "And if that's the case, I'm afraid I can't help you. You see, the designer built a virus into the program. It actually attacks the players who use stolen copies of the program."

"What?" I gasped. "That can't be legal!"

"Neither is a bootleg disk," said the voice. "If that's what you're playing, you're doomed."

The phone crackled and went dead.

14

Out of Control

What a night!

I felt like one of those magicians who starts dozens of plates spinning on stage, then has to run around to keep them going.

After Ben left, I parked myself at the computer. After the tip from the woman on the phone, I decided to learn everything I could about level five. But my father's limiting my computer time made that tricky. If he poked his head in, I planned to tell him that I'd just booted up.

Meanwhile, there was Thor. It's not easy to keep a seven-foot gladiator quiet. Especially when he's leaning over your shoulder, trying to tell you how to play a game.

You get the picture.

Add to that the fact that level five, Final Quest, was one of the weirdest games I'd ever played.

The player rode in a tiny capsule for a voyage through the human body. You had to go to the heart to defend your emotions. Then you went to the brain to defend your thoughts. Then you traveled to the soul—actually, the sole of your foot—to defend your beliefs.

The graphics were psychedelic. The wild colors reminded me of tie-dyed T-shirts.

The phantoms appeared as creepy disease cells and black viruses that attacked your capsule. There were also fat globules that could block your way to the next station.

Let's face it. The person who'd dreamed up this game must have been totally Fruit Loops. But Thor seemed to like it. He especially liked the questions you had to answer in each station before you could move on. And when it came to the brain teasers, Thor was surprisingly good.

In my voyage, I found a key tangled up in some nerves. I managed to free it and added it to the cargo hold of my capsule. "Maybe it unlocks a door," I said aloud.

"Good thinking," Thor agreed. "A key to the back door. But where is the door? It could be anywhere in the entire human body."

I sighed as my capsule plunged back into the bloodstream. We needed a tip. I wished that woman at the Shadow Zone hot line had told me more, but she seemed to know I had a bootleg disk.

"What did that woman on the hot line say?" I asked Thor.

"That you're doomed?"

I shook my head. "That level five was the designer's favorite...because it's the only level with a heart! Let's take a look in the heart."

Our vessel sped from one artery to another, until finally we reached the giant red pump.

Thor was the first to spot it, inside one chamber. "There...there's a door!" he said.

My heart was racing as our vessel swam over to the door. The key fit! But once the door was open, our capsule was too big to go through the opening.

"Bummer!" I said, banging on the computer table just as someone knocked on the door.

"Hide!" I whispered.

Thor backed into the closet door and flattened himself into poster form just as my dad poked his head in.

"Mike, what did I say about your computer time?" Dad's face was stern.

"I know, two hours on the computer." I forced a smile. "I just turned it on this minute."

"Have you done your homework?" My father came up behind me and bent down to peer at the screen. "What on earth is that?" he asked, resting his hand on the monitor.

"A new game. And I was just about to start my home—"

Dad wrenched his hand from the top of the computer. "Michael, this computer is hot. Too hot to have just been turned on. How long have you been playing?"

"Half an hour?" I lied.

"Just turned it on, hmm?" My father shook his head. "You may play for thirty minutes more. I'll be back to check on you."

"Yes, sir."

"And I ran into Mrs. Gantry out in the driveway," Dad went on. "She said she saw you and Ben at the shopping center this afternoon. And that you were walking around with a guy dressed like some cartoon hero. Is this true?"

Isn't it amazing how rumors spread?

My stomach was in knots the next morning as Thor and I walked to school. I'd brought this curse on, so I had to find a way to undo it.

I hadn't found the password, and I didn't know what to expect when I arrived at school. After all, Ben, Thor, and I had stood the three phantoms up yesterday. I had a feeling they'd be ticked off.

From a few blocks away, I could see that the school parking lot was empty. There were no teachers' cars. Only a handful of kids waited at the edge of the schoolyard, afraid to get too close to the building.

Woodmont Middle School was like a ghost town. Thor and I stopped in front of the double doors.

"Something is very wrong," I said.

Thor lifted his hands toward the school and frowned. "There's a lot of electricity bouncing around inside. I can feel it."

What the heck did that mean?

One of the kids from the playground came toward us. It was Ben. His face was drawn and his eyes were puffy, as if he hadn't slept too well last night.

"Did you find the password?" he asked.

I shook my head. "No such luck."

"Well, it's probably too late, anyway. John Miluski's been inside." Ben nodded toward the school. "He says we won't recognize the place."

"What did the phantoms do?" I asked.

"Beats me," said Ben. "That's all I could squeeze out of John before he tore down the street."

"Let's take a look," Thor said, turning toward the doors. I was glad he was willing to go in ahead of me.

Inside, the squeak of our sneakers echoed through the empty hall. As we passed the office, the clock sounded so loud. *Tick-tick-tick...*

The Bear didn't stop us. Mrs. Wu's desk was empty. The building was quiet—dead quiet.

"Where is everyone?" I whispered.

"The kids who didn't get zapped yesterday decided to stay home today," Ben explained. "Same with the teachers. They may have tried to call in sick, but no one was here to answer the phones."

"Gym class is going to be a drag," Thor said, checking out the empty halls.

"There won't *be* any gym class." I looked past a row of lockers. Not even the leanest, bravest jocks had dared to show up. The whole school had jumped ship.

When we turned the corner near the cafeteria, Thor stopped.

"Electricity...I can feel it in there." He went toward the lunchroom door.

"Careful, man," Ben whispered as Thor tugged the door open and blinked.

It was an amazing sight—an animated circus.

"Wow..." I gasped as Ben and I moved into the doorway beside Thor.

Creatures and characters from every video game I'd ever played had come to life. And they were zipping and banging and bouncing around in our school lunch room.

Retro-rockets whirred through the air.

Race cars roared in circles.

A paintbrush the size of a baseball bat splashed paint on the concrete wall.

Super Sleuths snooped under the tables and chairs. Their spy glasses combed the floor, collecting dust samples and lost buttons.

Pack-Rats had invaded the food supply. They were swarming over torn bags of bread, munching like maniacs.

Alien pods were embedded in the lunch tables. As I watched, a squadron of purple aliens waddled out of a pod. Moving in formation, they turned toward us and raised their prickly wings.

Suddenly, the hair on the back of my neck stood on end. I'd fought those aliens before.

"Look out!" I shouted. "They're going to fire!"

15

Phantom Frenzy

I grabbed Thor and Ben, and we all ducked—right in the nick of time!

The aliens fired a stream of death rays over our heads. When the dust had cleared, there were a hundred tiny holes in the steel door behind us.

"Unbelievable..." Ben said.

"Where did these creatures come from?" asked Thor. "Level two? Level three?"

I shook my head. "They're not even from the *Phantom Quest* game," I explained. "Siren and the others must have gone into the school computer and brought out creatures from every game on the hard drive. They're all from harmless computer games."

"They're not harmless anymore," Ben said. "I say we get out of here before something else comes after us."

Thor held the door open while we rushed

out, then shut it firmly behind us.

"Unbelievable," Ben repeated. "That room is like watching thousands of scrambled computer games."

"Do you like our pets?"

I froze at the sound of Siren's voice.

"Don't look now," Ben muttered, "but I think the three stooges are here."

Slowly I turned and saw the three gladiators standing in front of the lockers.

"We were pleased to find so many creatures in the computer," Mongo said. His bug eyes shone like marbles.

"We worked with them all night long." Siren let out a dramatic yawn. "They had to be trained, of course."

"Now they obey us," Exterminator said. "They follow our commands. Unlike some *kids* we know."

Ben and I looked at each other. They were ticked off. We were going to fry. Sizzle. Pop.

"Back off," Thor growled at them. "These kids are still on my team."

"Some team," Mongo snorted. "You didn't even show up for yesterday's tournament."

"We had other things to do," Thor said, tossing it off lightly. "You want to have a match? Let's do it. Right now."

A match? I swallowed hard. Thor's brain had to be turning to mist.

Mongo licked his lips eagerly, but Siren shook her head.

"The tournament is off," she snapped.

"We have found a better use for these kids." Exterminator smiled at us, and for a moment I wondered if his gray teeth were made of steel. Or was that tooth decay?

"Why do I feel like a caged animal?" Ben muttered.

"It's that darned computer," Mongo whined.

"We've discovered a...problem," Exterminator said. "We can't go far from the *Phantom Quest* program. We're stuck here in this rather boring level."

"It's called a school," Ben said heatedly. "At least, it used to be."

"We need to branch out. We've got an army now," Mongo said, pointing to the cafeteria where the cartoon creatures were zooming around. "We've got the strength. And we've got the power."

"Power is easy to find. It's everywhere." To prove her point, Siren leaped up and grabbed the overhead light. As she recharged, she reminded me of a red stop light. Then she dropped back to the floor at our feet.

"But we need more freedom to move about," Exterminator said. "Tell us, Thor. How is it that *you* can travel wherever you please?"

My hand tightened over the strap of my knapsack. The game disk was inside. I couldn't let them get their hands on it.

"Share your secret," Siren hissed.

"Do you have a portable computer?" Mongo asked. "Or is there some trick in the program?"

Thor scratched his chin thoughtfully, then smiled. "It's a trick. There's a way to put the program in a capsule and carry it with you."

The three phantoms stepped toward us.

"Really?" Siren purred.

Mongo's wet lips quivered. "Show us!"

"We'll do better than that." Thor put a beefy hand on my shoulder. "Mikey will make capsules for all of you."

The phantoms cooed, delighted at the offer. Suddenly, they eyed me as if I were a giant box of chocolates.

I was hurt and frightened. Thor had betrayed Ben and me. And although I didn't know exactly what the phantoms intended to do once they got their freedom, I did know it wouldn't be anything good. Let's put it this way, they weren't going to go out and join the scouts.

"But the capsules come with a price," Thor

said. "You must agree not to harm my team." He glared at Mongo, adding, "No zaps. No shocks. I don't want to see a single spark fly toward either of them."

"Too bad," Mongo said, staring at me. "I'd love to zap the little one who used to play the game incessantly."

"There's a whole world of children to zap," Siren reminded him. She turned to Thor. "We agree to your bargain."

"You have our promise," Exterminator added.

"Good." Thor clapped his big hands together. "Then let's get started."

"Traitor," Ben mumbled under his breath.

"How long will it take to make the capsules?" Siren asked.

As far as I was concerned, the phantoms could wait a hundred years before I'd lift a finger to help them.

"There's no way to tell," Thor answered. "Mike will start working on it right away. We'll keep you posted. Come on, guys," he said, dragging Ben and me away.

"That gives us more time to drill the army," Exterminator said gleefully.

Siren tugged open the lunchroom door, and three Super Sleuths spilled out. "Get back inside, you nosy clowns!"

"*You* can train *them*," Mongo whined. "This time, *I* get to play with the alien pods."

I turned away and concentrated on keeping up with Thor. He was still pulling me by the arm. The guy was really hustling as we turned a corner.

"What's the hurry?" I snapped. "The phantoms have already ruined the school. Do they get bonus points for trashing the town by sundown?"

"Really," Ben agreed, shaking Thor off. "You sold us out in seconds flat. What's your problem, bud? Haven't you ever heard of loyalty?"

That made Thor pause. "I'm hurt."

"Excuse me?" Ben snapped.

"You guys got me all wrong. I would never give up my team."

"So what was all that about?" I asked, pointing behind me.

"I was bluffing," Thor admitted. "It was the only way out."

Ben and I exchanged a look of surprise. Then we both smiled.

"Nice going, Thor," Ben said, clapping him on the back. "You're finally beginning to catch on to reality."

Thor smiled. "Thanks, bud. I have a—" He paused. "Do you hear that?"

A faint, willowy voice echoed down the hall. "Help! Someone help me..."

We bolted up to the main corridor and looked both ways. On the right side, dark figures swarmed at the end of the hall.

"Help me! Please!"

"What's going on?" Ben asked, squinting down the corridor.

It was a girl, and she sounded desperate. Swallowing my fear, I raced ahead. I was halfway down the hall before I could make out her face.

It was Vickie Goldberg. She was being chased by Pack-Rats! They scampered along at her heels, nipping at her skirt.

"Mike, help me!" Tears streamed down her cheeks.

She stumbled for a second, and one Pack-Rat caught up with her. It crawled up her back and sank its claws in her thick brown hair.

Vickie screamed.

As I watched in horror, the rat perched on her shoulder and began to gnaw on her hair!

16

Pack-Rat Attack

"Push them away!" I shouted to her. "Don't let them know you're scared. We'll help you."

Gritting her teeth, Vickie reached back and swatted at the Pack-Rat. She missed once, then managed to knock it loose. The rat bounced to the floor with a squeak.

"Get lost!" I ran forward and kicked away two of the rats that were nipping at Vickie's skirt.

Ben knocked away two others with one swing of his knapsack.

Then came Thor—with a fire extinguisher. He rolled it down the hall toward a row of Pack-Rats.

Wham!

Like a group of bowling pins, the rats went flying. That sent the rest of them scampering away. Their squeals died out as they fled into a dark classroom.

"Thanks, guys," Vickie said. "I was afraid

they'd eat me alive." She shook out her hair and shuddered. I could see where Pack-Rats had chewed holes in the back of her suede jacket.

"I thought the three stooges had them trained," Ben said.

"Looks like Larry, Moe, and Curly aren't the best teachers in the world," I added.

Thor frowned. "If those creatures get out of this building, reality is going to be a mess."

"Chaos," I agreed.

"An organized chaos," Vickie said. "Those gladiators are planning to take over the world, starting with the town of Woodmont."

"Why doesn't that surprise me?" Ben said, rolling his eyes.

"How do you know?" I asked Vickie.

"I heard them talking. I just came into the building to get my jacket. I forgot it yesterday. But then I heard the three phantoms talking in a classroom. They'd pulled down the geography map. There was a little circle around Illinois. I guess they figured out where we are. They were numbering the states. You know, deciding what order to attack them in."

"That's why they need to be more mobile," I said. "So they can take over the whole country."

"Zapping anyone who gets in their way," said Ben. "Pretty soon half of the world population will be inside the *Phantom Quest* game."

And I would be the one who caused it all. The boy who couldn't tear himself away from a computer game. I'd be famous—only my name would be lumped together with criminals like Jesse James, Al Capone, and Ted Bundy.

"We've got to stop them," I said. "There has to be a way..."

"I have an idea," Thor said. "But we'll need to use the computer, and you'll have to stall the phantoms for a while."

"We can hold 'em off!" Ben said.

"And you'd better find a safe place to hide," Thor said, patting Vickie's shoulder. "Siren and the others promised not to hurt the boys, but I won't be able to protect you."

"Gotcha," Vickie nodded. "I'm out of here."

We walked her to the end of the hall, and Thor held the exit door open for her.

"I'm going to lock all the doors and windows and close the blinds when I get home." She smiled as she tucked her hair behind her ears. "Good luck, you guys."

I watched until Vickie disappeared behind the oak trees across the street. Then I joined Thor and Ben, who were already booting up a terminal in the computer lab.

"So what's the plan?" I asked.

"You're going to send me into the computer to look for the password," Thor said.

"What?" I frowned. "You said you were bored with level four. Besides, what if we can't get you back out?"

"I think I've found the place where I belong." Thor's eyes glowed. "I'm going into level five— the Final Quest. I want to know what's inside that door in the heart. The capsule won't fit through the door—but I can!"

I had to admit, it wasn't a bad idea. When we'd played last night, Thor had really gotten into it. "We'll have to pick up that diver's suit that was hanging in that closet in the brain," I said, thinking aloud. "If you're suited up, you should make it."

"What are you two talking about?" Ben asked.

"Just watch." Quickly, I worked through the first three levels. When I got to level four, the gladiator choices went on and on. There were countless faces of teachers and students staring out at me.

"Unbelievable," Ben said as I scrolled through a few screens of faces. "They must have zapped half of our school."

Trying to ignore the sad looks on the kids' faces, I played my way to level five. "Okay," I said, looking up at Thor. "What next?"

"Get us to the screen that says *Choose your voyager,*" Thor said. "Then type in my name."

I did as he instructed. T-H-O-R.

"Okay." He squared off a few feet from the computer and raised his hands. "Wish me luck," he said, pointing at the screen.

"Go for it," I said.

"Let 'er rip!" Ben said cheerfully.

Ben and I covered our eyes as Thor zapped the computer. There was a bright flash. Then Thor was gone, leaving a trail of green smoke.

"Unbelievable!" Ben gasped.

"Say that one more time and I'll send *you* into the game," I told Ben.

He grinned. "Sorry, bud."

Just then a wisp of smoke curled out of the computer's hard drive. Had Thor's trick backfired?

"Uh-oh," Ben said as the smoke snaked into the shape of a man. But it wasn't tall enough to be Thor. This man was shorter. His hair was dark. His grin was lean and mean.

"Coach Rocco!" Ben smacked his forehead.

"That's right! He took Thor's place in the computer. Now that Thor is in, the coach is out."

Coach Rocco snapped to life. "Mr. Willis and Mr. Huxley." He wrinkled his nose at the surroundings. "I...You two had better..." Confused, he paused. "Why am I here?" he asked.

He didn't seem to remember being zapped—or spending the last twenty-four hours playing *Phantom Quest.*

"Just saying hello," Ben chirped. "But, uh, school is closed today. And you're already late for your tennis match at the club."

The coach didn't seem convinced, but he didn't fight it. "Fine. See you two in gym class."

As he went out the door, I asked Ben, "Do you think we ought to escort him out?"

Ben went to the door and peered down the hall. "He's okay. Just ducking out the exit."

I scooted up to the computer. "Now, let's see if Thor's plan worked."

I went to the voyager screen on level five, and Thor was there! His blond head filled the window of the capsule. I selected Thor for Final Quest, and the game began.

"Can you hear us?" I asked aloud.

His voice was distorted, but it came through. "Gotcha, Mikey!"

"You need to pick up the wet suit in the brain, then the key that's tangled in the nerves," I instructed.

Thor's capsule sped off toward the brain.

"Come on, buddy!" Ben cheered. "Head out for the back door. Pass the word to the nerds!"

You could always count on Ben to make the most of a moment.

We waited as Thor picked up the tools he needed. The whole thing was kind of nerve-racking. Since I had to let Thor call the shots, I felt helpless. And Ben was antsy. He stood up and paced back and forth behind me.

"Mikey," Thor's voice crackled at last. "I'm swimming out to open the door."

All right! I thought, sagging with relief.

"Uh, Mikey," Ben said. "I think you'd better—"

"Not now, Ben," I said. "Thor's going in the door. What's inside, Thor?"

"A banner. It says, *The quest begins...*"

"How's it going? Finished yet? Where's Thor?" The barrage of questions came from Siren. She was right behind me.

I pushed away from the computer. I'd have to wing it. "Um, not yet. We were just—"

"Where's Thor?" she demanded. Her dark eyes roved the room, then honed in on the monitor. "In there! He's in the game." She laughed.

"It's the...uh...process," I said lamely.

Ben rushed over to block the screen. "This is an important stage. You shouldn't be here."

"Ha!" she snapped. "This is the chance I've been waiting for!" She pointed her long finger-nails at the screen. I thought she was going to zap the computer and somehow get Thor.

But she didn't have a chance because Ben jumped in the way. The red sparks hit him smack in the chest.

Then he crumpled over...and vanished!

17

A Back Door

"Ben!" I shouted. I lunged at Siren, knocking her hands aside.

"Why did you do that?" I demanded. "You promised Thor that you wouldn't hurt us...and a gladiator never breaks a promise."

"Ha! Those are the rules of level four. Now we're playing a different game." She smiled at me. "You're the only one we need to keep, at least until you make us those capsules."

"I'll never help you!" I cried. "Never!" I ran out the door and tore down the hall.

I knew Siren would be right behind me, but I didn't think she would zap me. Without me, the three phantoms would never be able to travel far from this building. They needed me alive, at least for now.

But how was I going to escape?

I whipped around the corner and saw Mongo in the school office. He was stretched out on

Mrs. Wu's desk, his body a glowing purple mound. His toes were stuck into the wall socket, and he hummed softly.

"Wake up, you idiot!" Siren called to him. "Stop the kid!"

But Mongo was too slow.

My heart was pounding. I wasn't used to running, but my legs just kept pumping.

At the end of the hall was my target. The exit door.

But just as I had gotten to the home stretch, Exterminator stepped out of the cafeteria door. Spotting me, he stationed himself between me and the door. His arms were crossed, his feet spread apart. His posture said, *You'll never get past me.*

Thinking fast, I dove to the ground and slid. My sweater moved smoothly along the polished floor. In a few seconds, I was zipping through Exterminator's legs and right up to the exit door.

Too scared to look back, I scrambled to my feet and threw myself against the door. It popped open, and I was outside in the cool air!

Breathing heavily, I ran to the back of the school and found the stairwell that led down to the basement. From time to time, I'd seen the school janitors coming and going from this entrance. But for me, this was strange territory.

Kids never went into the school basement.

Until now.

I tugged open the steel door, stepped into the shadows, and flicked the light switch.

The big, hollow room was surprisingly empty. No cobwebs or creaky stairs here. Just a plain cement floor and exposed pipes.

I crept past the furnace, searching for the one thing that could stall the phantoms. It had to be down here somewhere!

At last, I spotted the gray metal box on the wall. The fuse box!

The electrical system was labeled. Lucky for me. I found the main switch and turned the lever to the "off" side.

That would cut off the phantoms' power, and in a little while their energy would wind down. It would give me some time to think. But I couldn't leave the power off forever. Dozens of people—including Ben—were trapped in that computer upstairs. I couldn't just turn off the power and walk away. I had to get the people out.

How was I going to fix things without Ben?

I brushed my hands on my jeans and sat down on an old crate. Too bad Siren had walked in just when Thor found the back door. What had he said?

"The quest begins..." I said aloud. When? In the morning? At midnight? Or maybe it was a place.

I came up with dozens of combinations. So many, I was starting to drive myself nuts. "The quest begins...in your brother's dirty socks."

Just then the door creaked open. My head whipped around; someone was standing in the light that streamed in from outside.

"Mike?" she called.

It was Vickie Goldberg.

"Over here."

She let the door shut and joined me. "I saw you run down here. What's happening?"

"I thought you were going straight home."

She shrugged. "I was curious. I waited and watched from behind the oak trees across the street. Where's Ben?"

I rubbed my eyes and sighed. "He got zapped."

"Oh, no!" She covered her mouth with her hands. "That's awful."

"And Thor's in the computer. He found part of the password," I told her. Then I explained everything that had gone on.

I kicked at a scrap of wood on the floor. "And all this is my fault. Because I played a stupid computer game."

"Don't blame yourself," she said. "The way I see it, it was bound to happen to someone. I think everyone in Woodmont is lucky that you were the one, Mike. Lots of other kids would be too chicken to do what you're doing. You're risking everything to save people."

That made me feel better. Maybe I wouldn't be blamed for ruining the world. Maybe my mug shot wouldn't be on *America's Most Wanted*.

"So what's next?" Vickie asked.

I frowned. "I'll switch the power on and try to locate Thor again. I've got to work fast. And if you don't mind, there's something you can do to help..."

"Okay, magic fingers, let's play," I whispered.

I was sitting in the computer lab, waiting for the power to come on. Vickie had agreed to count to one hundred, then throw the switch. That way, I could move into place before any of the phantoms materialized.

My fingers were poised over the keyboard when the lights flickered on. The computer booted up...and my fingers raced over the keys as I quickly skipped ahead until I reached level five.

"Thor!" I called, checking all the vessels. "Where are you?"

"Mikey..." The voice was faint, and I couldn't tell where it was coming from. Thinking fast, I grabbed a vessel and raced toward the heart, where I'd left him.

I found him there, swimming around outside the door. "Thor! Did you see the password?"

"Yes!" he shouted. "The message is: *The quest—*"

"Back again?" Exterminator's voice cut in. The hair on the back of my neck rose, but I refused to let him see that I was scared.

"Play the game." He chuckled. "Then die."

Thor was still shouting. His words were garbled, but I thought I got the message.

Ignoring Exterminator's hot breath, I pressed CONTROL, ALT, and DELETE at the same time. The screen went black, then I typed the password Thor gave me: *The quest begins within.*

As I hit ENTER, I saw orange sparks fly past my ear. Exterminator was trying to zap me!

"Yikes!" I managed to roll my chair to the side, out of the path of electricity.

When I looked back at the monitor, there was the *Phantom Quest* logo. I felt a surge of hope. Had the password worked? Had I cured the virus?

The air in the room began to move as if a storm wind was coming. We had tornadoes in

Illinois, but as far as I knew they didn't start inside buildings.

Exterminator yelped as he backed toward the doorway. "No! Stop!" he shouted, clinging to the steel frame.

I gripped the edge of a desk, trying to resist the tug of the wind.

Papers, pencils, and dust flew through the room. They danced around in a wide circle as the air began to churn. Everything was being sucked into the computer.

Everything...including me!

18

Sucked Up

"Look what you've done!" Exterminator cried. "The vortex! It's going to swallow us—all of us!"

Speak for yourself, bud. I wasn't giving up now!

I gripped the desk. My fingernails dug into the wood surface as I pulled my body away from the sucking wind. I managed to swing my legs into the kneehole of the desk. Then I jammed them apart so that my sneakers gripped the wood. That would hold me, for now.

But Exterminator wasn't so lucky.

The power outage had weakened him, and the wind was strong. As I watched, his steely fingernails scraped along the door frame, peeling off lines of paint. He let out a bone-chilling scream as the wind wrenched him loose.

I watched in awe as the huge man spun cartwheels through the air and tumbled toward the computer. In a second, he was sucked in.

But the churning vortex didn't let up. Other creatures were dragged into the room by the sucking wind.

Squealing Pack-Rats rolled by like tumbleweed. Retro-rockets zipped in the door and fired a last burst of smoke. The alien pods flew through the air. Every computer creature that had come out was now going back in.

Like a giant vacuum, the computer sucked them all up.

Siren and Mongo were the last to go. They skidded into the room at the same time, their arms flailing against the wind.

"It's the vortex!" Mongo shouted.

"You did this!" Siren shrieked at me. She pointed her red fingernails at me.

There was no way I could duck. I was holding onto the desk, using all my energy to resist the wind.

Red sparks shot out from Siren's fingertips. But the wind pulled the electricity, too, until it swirled around her. She looked like a cherry Danish.

The wind roared. Its power was too much for the weakened gladiators. Their screams were sucked into the vacuum as they somersaulted into the computer.

Me? I was still holding on with all my might.

I had decided that I definitely wanted to stay in reality. Even if that meant listening to my parents and doing homework and not playing computer games in class. I wanted to stay here and hang with Ben and Vickie and the other kids at Woodmont Middle School.

As soon as Siren and Mongo were gone, the wind began to let up. Paper and dust glided to the floor like falling leaves.

Then the wind itself was gone. And so were the phantoms.

I took a deep breath, as the computer spit out a few puffs of smoke. This is it! I thought, wheeling my chair around to face the computer. Please send back Ben!

The smoke kept coming. Each cloud grew until it swirled into the shape of a person—a human person.

One by one, teachers and kids sparked to life around me. Mrs. Fernandez smiled down at me in a dazed way. The Bear raked his fingers through his bushy beard, looking a little confused. And Mr. Norman stretched as if he'd just woken up from a long nap.

Stephanie and the other kids looked around curiously.

"Were we just on *Totally Hidden Videos*?" one kid asked.

"Not exactly," I said, looking through the smoky ranks of people. Where was Ben?

Someone touched my shoulder. I spun around and stared into a pair of round brown eyes.

"Benarooni!" I gave him a hug, which seemed to really confuse him.

"Easy, man," he muttered under his breath. "There are H.B. watching."

Hot babes? "Sorry." I released him. "I'm just glad to see you."

"Me, too. I guess." He ran a hand over his flat top. "What are all these people doing here?"

"It's a long story," I told him quietly. "I'll explain it after we get rid of them. But I'm not sure what to say. There's no school today. Maybe we should tell them it's because the power went out..."

"No school?" Ben grinned. "Bonus." He turned to the crowd, a big smile on his face. "Okay, folks. School has been canceled for the day due to the power failure. You can all go home now."

"But it looks as if the power is back on," Mr. Borinski said, pointing to the computer monitor. "That means we'll see each and every one of you tomorrow morning." He looked down at me, adding, "On time, please."

"Yes, sir," I said.

Everyone started filing out of the computer lab. Quickly, I sat down at the terminal and finished off what I had to do. I erased the *Phantom Quest* game from the school's hard drive and from the disk that Hacker had given me.

I have to admit, I felt a little bad after I typed in that last command. I couldn't help but wonder what would happen to Thor. Did he like level five? I wished that I could make sure he was okay, but there was no way I could keep the bootleg copy of this game around.

Ben took a chair beside me. As I worked, I filled in the blanks of his Swiss-cheesed memory. He was pretty impressed by the whole story.

"We're heroes, Mikey!" he said, clapping me on the back.

"You sure are!" came a voice from the doorway. Vickie Goldberg tucked a curl behind one ear and gave us both a big smile. "I saw all those people out in the corridor. You did it! You saved the school!"

"You helped," I told her. "Thanks for staying down in the basement to throw the switch."

"No problem."

As we talked, Ben nudged my arm. "Uhm, Mikey. Looks like someone left you a message." He pointed at the computer screen.

There was a note there, typed up just like a letter you'd get in the mail.

> Dear Mikey,
> Thanks, bud! Level five is full of surprises. I think I'm going to be happy here.
> Enjoy reality. And don't get all corny about missing me. I'll always be here, in my capsule on level five. Only next time, buy a copy of the game. Those bootleg disks can give your computer a nasty virus.
> Later, dude!
>
> Thor

"Would you look at that," Ben said. "A message from the computer abyss."

I sighed. It was good to know that Thor had gotten what he wanted. "And that's going to be the last contact we have with *anything* from the other side of the screen."

"Well," Vickie said, plopping into a chair. "I've been meaning to talk to you guys about that. I don't know where else to turn."

"Uh-oh." Ben sighed.

"What do you mean, Vick?" I asked.

"There's this game called *The Core*. I have it at home," she explained. "It's about the creatures who stoke the fires at the center of the earth."

"I've heard of it," I admitted. "What's the problem?"

"Well..." she hesitated. "It's not a bootleg or anything. I mean, my dad bought it for me the last time he was on a business trip in South America. But every time I get to level four, my room starts to heat up...."

Don't miss the next book in the
Shadow Zone series:
THE UNDEAD EXPRESS

Valentine leaned even closer. "Not *dead* people. *Un*dead."

I couldn't have heard right. "What did you say?"

"The *Undead*," Valentine repeated. He spread his arms to include everyone in the subway car. His eyes seemed to burn with a steady fire. "We are not alive. We are not dead. But we feed on the blood of the living."

Okay, I'm a city kid. I've got street smarts. But even though I *knew* this crazy guy was just trying to shake me up, I couldn't ignore it. I was scared.

"What are you nervous about, Zachary?" Valentine hissed softly. "Don't you know about the *nosferatu?*"

"The nose-for-*what?*" I asked, trying to joke away my fear. Then my blood ran cold. "Hey, wait a second. How did you know my name?"

"*Nosferatu*, Zachary," Valentine repeated. "The undead. We are all vampires...And we'd like to welcome you to the Undead Express!"